REPLENISHING JESSICA

AMS PRESS
NEW YORK

Replenishing Jessica

MAXWELL BODENHEIM

Frederick Fell, Inc.

NEW YORK

1949

Library of Congress Cataloging in Publication Data

Bodenheim, Maxwell, 1893-1954.
  Replenishing Jessica.

  Reprint of the 1925 ed. published by H. Liveright,
New York.
  I. Title
PZ3.B6317Re7   [PS3503.O17]   813'.5'2   73-18548
ISBN 0-404-11363-X

PS
3503
O17
R38
1974

From the impression of 1949, New York
First AMS edition published in 1975
Manufactured in the United States of America

AMS PRESS INC.
NEW YORK, N. Y. 10003

PART ONE

REPLENISHING JESSICA

PART ONE

SOMETIMES rooms are filled with all of the words that people do not say to each other. The unspoken words hang in the air, like an impalpable contradiction, or else they hover in a richly unseen friendliness that strengthens the more faltering sounds from the lips of the speakers. The man and woman in the room feel this presence and often help it with their silences

Jessica Maringold joined a silence of this kind as she let her hands drop while they were in the midst of playing one of Satie's light affairs. She slumped down on the piano bench, with her arms between her knees, and her hands clasped. She was a little above medium height, with a body that was quite plump between the hips and upper thighs. Elsewhere, it narrowed and tapered off to a remarkable slenderness, but so gradually that the grace of lines was not hindered. A young poet, whom she had met in a tea room, had once written that her hair was "like a transfigured midnight," and a dryly bluish glint showed upon the blackness. Her skin was a pale brown that almost receded into white. She had a straight nose, barely tilted at the tip, small, thin

9

lips that did not seem to be sensual until you had looked at them for a long time, and a chin that was daintily determined. Her eyes were large and black, and in its entirety her face was one quarter of an inch removed from absolute prettiness, thus avoiding the insipid air attached to over-symmetrical countenances. As she bent over the piano keys, her face had an odd look——lightly hurt, discontented, distracted.

Theodore Purrel sat near her and smoked a cigar. He was a tall man, just above thirty years, and he had the body of an athlete beginning to deteriorate ——the first sign of a paunch and too much fat on his legs. He had much dark brown hair and it was smoothly oiled down, a fashion observed by men who believe that they cannot look rakish without presenting a sleekly unnatural appearance. His face was too plump above its bold jaw and his nose was unbroken and diminutive. A certain femininity contended with the masculine elements of his face, which strove to look ferocious in a subconscious effort to dispel their foe. He had a small, brown mustache and small, brown eyes, and moderately thick lips puffed out a bit. As he sat beside Jessica, the room was filled with the words of physical cajolery and invitation which he had not spoken in spite of his desires, while Jessica was thinking of Salburg, the artist, and of the perversely martyred boredom that seemed to be in his eyes, and of whether it was real or merely an expedient used to snare the attention

of women. Sometimes a vision of Purrel intruded
upon her thoughts, and then she told him inaudibly
to visit a cabaret and pick up a fat, lecherous woman
and remain in his world. The music room was a
different world and he was bothering it with obvious
longings and a raillery whose main sidesteppings she
had long since memorized. She turned quickly on
the bench, her thoughts dispersed by his humming
of a popular tune.

"Go home, Ted," she said, in a voice that was
pleading but cool.

"If I thought you were going to finish that Satie
stuff, I would," he answered. "I don't know what
you see in those modern composers. When they have
something that sounds like a melody—and it's not
often—they proceed to break it up with endless
screeches and a lot of fussing on the upper scales."

"Yes, I know, and you'll take jazz every time,"
she said. "And come on, let's drop into The Painted
Tent and finish the night with a ba-a-ang. Not tonight, Ted."

"You've got one of your highbrow moods," he
announced. "It always starts with you breaking
off in the middle of a piece. Then you sit and look
mysterious and think you're putting it over."

"If I'm not putting it over, perhaps you'll tell
me what I'm thinking about," she said, with a vestige
of hope that he might surprise her.

"You were back in your kid days, picking daisies
for mother," answered Purrel. "Sure, that's it."

"Wise-cracking" was Purrel's main refuge. It was invaluable for the purpose of insinuating that you knew something which, in reality, had not lodged in your head. It offered your ignorance the balm of derisively symbolizing an explanation which could not possibly be true, and in this process your ignorance became intelligent in its own estimation. You knew what the thing was not, and what it was must be at the other extreme. Sure. Again, "wise-cracking" was a clog-dance indulged in by the heavy, hoggish sameness of your thoughts and emotions. Somehow, the recurrences had to be broken up with smart, glib words that could give them an uppish, varied fling (you're the bee's mustache; the beetle's bandanna; the turtle's requiem; come on, unfold yourself, kid; breeze out, oldtimer, you're coming apart; you whisper it, I'm paralyzed, etc.). He kept on dodging Jessica's remarks, with an imagistic bantering. As she talked to him she wondered at her patience.

She had dismissed men who were much more intelligent than he was, and the elephantine shiftings of his mind bored her because they tried so hard to be surreptitious, yet she allowed him to see her at least once and often twice during the course of a week. Was it because she liked the half-practiced and half-boyish way in which his hands and lips touched her skin? He was curious in one respect—that his body seemed to be infinitely more alive and thoughtful than his words, or his brain. When he stroked and kissed her, his lips and fingers were filled with the subtlest of pranks, with a poem in which light and heavy pressures were almost æsthetically placed and proportioned. His caresses always stopped just before the point where they would have become irksome and always continued at the moment when her body was signaling for their return. In his lovemaking he could become by turns supernaturally delicate and gracefully direct, and his embraces held a deliberateness so unerring that it seemed to rise to a higher spontaneity—a spontaneity free from all indecisions and gaucheries. It was almost as though all of Purrel's thought, emotion, and spirit were concealed in his flesh and waited for motion to release them and make them conscious. A new, entirely altered man clung to her and skillfully apologized for the stupidity of the first individual.

When Purrel was seated or walking beside her, his entire identity changed. He returned to an inanely talkative stockbroker immersed in a chase for money that was too vapid to be cruel, and advancing the tactics of a dull, self-confident libertine and "night-life" adventurer. His brain released hundreds of conventional, borrowed ideas; his limbs became awkward; his face was amusingly gross. Then she would resume the conversation with him, hoping that some stray remark of his would reveal a kinship with the silent self that had besieged her, and so often disappointed her that she had finally given him up as a mystery. Had she deluded herself in this matter? Was it possible that she had seized an ordinary efficiency on his part and altered it with the intensity of her desires, turning it to the possessive perfections which she craved? In that case, why had she been unable to accomplish this with any other man? The caresses of other men were often endurable, and sometimes satisfying for a moment, but their contacts were sensual and nothing else—no separate, distinguished dream came forth from them. Their love-making was always deeply inferior to their words and thoughts, whereas Purrel exactly reversed the situation.

She remembered the one night in which she had given herself to him. They had returned from a party at 3 A.M. and they were both in that state of tipsiness in which thought assumes a feathery clownishness and uses every opportunity to ingratiate itself with unclad emotions. Several cocktails had produced this condition and the only difference was that in Jessica it represented a careless descension from her usual self, whereas Purrel was merely pinching his customary spirit and telling it how quaintly perfect it was. They tiptoed into the front drawing-room of the house and stopped every three steps to remind each other that they were making explosive noises, for Jessica's father and a spinister aunt and various servants were sleeping upstairs and must not be awakened. After throwing their outer wraps on the floor, they sat on a couch and regarded each other. Purrel's face had an indolent, uncertain

grin, while Jessica looked silly, and wistful, and unconcerned, with all three expressions following each
other so closely that they seemed to be one. The
alcohol had given a huge impishness to her emotions,
and they were nervously waiting for the final decline
of her mind. She knew that Purrel would grasp her,
and she reflected on some way of merrily repulsing
him, such as pulling his tie, wrenching his nose, tick-
ling his ears.

Without a word, he embraced her and drew her
head beneath his chin. His arms and hands had
been gentle and she could easily have resisted them,
but robbed of the incentive that comes from tussling,
and surprised at the almost birdlike carefulness of
his touch, she had yielded to see what he would do
next. When he began to press her shoulders down
upon the couch she braced herself against him.

"What are you trying to do, Ted," she had said.
"Don't be foolish."

She had used the words more to rouse herself
from a fondling lethargy than from any effort to
dissuade him. She was still uncertain as to whether
she wanted him to take her and she was assigning to
him the burden of convincing her in one way or another. The grin had left his face and a fresh, charmingly adolescent impatience had replaced it.

"Sh, don't speak words," he had said, in a tone of
soft, grave warning. "Sh, mustn't. Words 'r no
good now. They don't see you and me and they're
tryin' to find us and we mustn't let them. They're

always botherin' ev'body, you know, an' here's fine chance to make them leave us alone. When they don' find you, you're not afraid to act like you want to, see? Don' talk, Jessie——sh!"

He began to kiss her face with an extraordinary lightness, as though he feared that he might disfigure it, and his hands remained on her shoulders and made no effort to become more intimate. This was exactly what she had not expected, and the piquant sensitiveness of his words had astounded her, and she had decided that this new Purrel deserved to be rewarded. In a situation of this kind, if the woman is to any extent shackled by a brain, her physical longings are apt to be powerless until this brain gives an impressed nod of permission. The appearance of this nod hinges upon whether the man has been innately or deliberately able to make his advances without crudely offending the alien judge within the woman's head. Jessica, feeling herself upon the last edge of yielding, had instinctively uttered an insincere question.

"Why do you want me?" she had whispered, as she reclined on the couch, with her hands uncertainly resting on his head.

" 'Cause you're ten times better'n me an' cause I want to make it more even," he had answered. "There's something in me that nobody sees 'cept you, nobody, an' you mustn't let it die. You mustn't, 'cause if you do, then I'll forget all 'bout it after a while."

When the love of women is not a form of hero-worship it is the startled unbending to a simple child which the man has concealed until his moment of final pleading. Jessica had yielded her body to Purrel with a feeling of tender, amused, and slightly mystified superiority.

After this episode she had felt irritated and ashamed, and when he had visited her again, with his shallow remarks and second-hand Broadway mannerisms, the feeling had become a definite disgust. Still, she had continued to see him because, if she had avoided him, it would have been confessing that she had made an ignominious mistake, and because she wanted to discover whether a second self within him would once more surprise her. With a vengeful feeling she had waited for another urging on his part and had said to herself, "He won't find it so easy this time." When he had striven to possess her again, she had allowed him to kiss her but had rejected his more amorous onslaughts and informed him that they would never reiterate the previous night. His lips and hands were too warmly potent to be entirely spurned, but she was determined not to surrender again to a man whose subsequent actions and words made the surrender seem over-credulous and ordinary.

Purrel had failed to believe her, of course, and had been able to see only two interpretations of her attitude. She was either waiting for an offer of marriage or thought that he would regard her too

casually if she instantly allowed him to follow up his
victory. He was not given to diagnosing his
thoughts and emotions and he could not explain the
transformation that came over him when he touched
her. He knew only that she made him feel dizzy,
and softly helpless, and subdued, and that he could
not "treat her rough" as he did other women. He
had a hidden, hang-dog respect for her mind, because it was a troublesome conundrum to him, but
that alone would not have restrained him. It was
simply that he shivered when he touched her, and
jibed at himself for doing it until the jibe became
fainter and fainter and died, and that his mind
swerved into an unusually sober trance, and that he
wanted her too much to risk any possible defeat of
his longings. But why? Oh, well, you always felt
that way when you ran up against your real mate.
Eventually he would have to ask her to marry him
if he couldn't get her in any other way. He recoiled
from marriage because it carried leaden responsibilities and browbeating restrictions, but you couldn't
hope to escape from it forever. In the meantime he
still wanted to find out whether there was not a
chance of breaking down her opposition.

As she sat on the piano bench, he walked up to her,
and kissed her. The touch of her cheek seemed to
spread over him and hem him in, as though it were
a heated, resistless cloud. She was no longer quite
a woman to him, but a superbly insolent provocation,
and he congratulated himself upon having dared to

touch her and upon having made himself equal to her through the contact. All of the tricks and confidences with which he assailed other women fell from him, and his emotions took on a gentle wariness and strove to confirm their precarious success. Jessica stopped him with a pleading indecision when his hands brushed against her bosom, and were about to loosen the gold brooch that held her black waist together below her throat.

"I don't want to struggle with you," she said. "You'll think I'm not in earnest and you'll only keep it up. I'll be frank and tell you something. I like you when you stop talking and come close to me, and I detest you otherwise. You never say a word that you've actually thought out in your mind, and you never dream, and you hate everything that's not convenient and regular. The only time you try to talk to me is when you touch me, and then you seem to be absolutely different. But I can't love a man who doesn't know himself or me—life isn't all hugging and kissing."

Purrel felt that Jessica was unfairly scoffing at the practical, sensible virtues that made him a man of affairs, and expecting him to be some kind of effeminate, insincere butterfly. He felt also that she was blustering and trying to awe him so that she might be better able to rule him afterwards, while in reality her mind, in certain respects, was inferior to his. She had a faster tongue and she could twist around a few things that she had read and heard from this "nutty" book and that person, but when it came to a knowledge of life and its facts she was far behind him. Besides, what had she ever done? She painted a picture now and then, and ran around with a bunch of hungry artists, and felt puffed up about it. If she were ever thrown on the street and forced to make her own living she would wilt in twenty-four hours. The smooth audacity of women and their easy words! Yet, beneath all of the braggings and consolations wrought by his conscious ego, Purrel had a feeling which he could not analyze or cope with. Miserable, quivering, receding in stature beneath each of Jessica's words, it had nothing to say to him and it was deaf to his own statements. A wordless discomfiture, it goaded him to an ever-increasing stream of self-defenses that could not cease because his spirit would have mutely crumpled up in their absence. What in hell was it anyway? He knew only that it was a formless heaviness and that it seemed to suck in all of his words and conceits and make them dead and obnoxious, for no distinct reason. He parried with it for a moment, trying to bring some shape to it. Was there something in this art and intellect bunk after all? There was a cocksure brightness in Jessica's speech that made all of his own retorts seem stuttering in comparison. Perhaps the world was really different from the way in which he saw it, and he might be missing something that other people had found. The word "something," which was the only one that he could devise, irritated him because it inferred that he must either be ignorant or be playing with a nonexistent weight. Aw, rats, the entire question was idiotic. He was simply beginning to get tired of the money side of it—he had about as much as he wanted— and he needed a new game to interest him. Perhaps he ought to run for a public office, or buy a string of horses, or become a theatrical producer. It was hard to get much of a kick out of life unless people were talking about you, and you saw your name in the papers, and you knew that you were powerful enough to affect thousands of men and women, instead of a few clerks, business competitors, flappers, and chorus girls. If he could win a unique woman like Jessica it would shove him along the road and send him to larger conquests.

He had been silent for three minutes while Jessica tapped one of the keys on the piano and regarded him with contending boredom and pity. Everything else had failed, and if the whipping that she had given him could not rouse him to a glimmer of humility or interesting defiance, then he was hopeless.

"I wish you'd give this mind stuff a rest," he said. "If you can think so much better than I can, why don't you go out and demonstrate it? It doesn't take much brains to smear a little paint on canvas and knock around with a bunch of long-haired muts. When you do something that everybody talks about, and make a name for yourself in some line, then you'll have a right to criticize me. I may not be a world-beater but I've run up a fat bank account in the last eight years, and you can't do *that* on an empty head."

"Yes you can," said Jessica, in a most wearily placid sing-song voice, as though she were hopelessly chiding a baby. "You learn the routine of some little business—any precocious child could do it—and then you find out the times for lying and telling the truth. You've simply got to be honest and dishonest at the same time, and you've got to know how to mix them up so that most people won't be able to tell them apart. That's all. All of this talk about psy-chol-o-gy and bra-a-ains in business makes me laugh. You don't need anything except an instinct for moving backward and forward at the right time, just as an animal knows when to attack and when to creep back in his hole. Some people have it and others haven't, that's all."

Purrel had an outraged feeling, and he wanted to rush into words of general recrimination concerning Jessica's own dependence upon the money-making abilities which she had sneered at. Without the three million dollars which her father had accumulated in the real estate business she would be worrying about the family wash and the grocery bill, with no time for uppish vaporings and fine talk. These women, how they loved to twiddle their thumbs at the stanch realities without which their entire lives would collapse! She had probably been dipping into the freak book of some weak-kneed sociologist and was rehashing some of the sentences under the impression that she was being smart and original. Yet, in spite of his anger, his physical longing for her cautioned him to "go slow" in his reply. If he rapped her vanity too hard she might turn her back, even though she cared for him. Women, especially those of her kind, were quicksilvery and pampered creatures and had to be gingerly and insincerely treated at certain crucial moments. What they wanted was an indirect agreement with their opinions, and a careful technique in your love-making, and the cardinal difference between your treatment of them and men was that you could use fists, or a loud voice, or an open hardness with the latter, while usually you held yourself back with women.

"Have it your own way—I'm an an-i-mal and you're the goddess of something or other," he said. "I don't see why you take the trouble to talk to a man as stupid as I am. You seem to think it's a crime for some one to rake in money, but that doesn't stop you from spending it, all right."

"You're not so stupid, Ted, but the stupid part of you always talks first and then the intelligent part's ashamed to contradict it," she answered. "There's something almost intellectual about your kisses, anyway."

"That's a rotten compliment," he said, confused and annoyed, and he kissed her in a vindictively inarticulate effort to regain his sense of power over her. Her mind scornfully asked her why she was yielding

to him, but the indifferent vortex of her heart refused to answer. What did this man have hidden
within him that could make her forget all of his
familiar, price-tagged words and give her a trapped,
quivering acquiescence?

His hand once more fumbled at the golden brooch
that held her waist together at the throat. He
touched her skin as though he expected it to vanish
at any moment and was begging it to remain. His
fingers enveloped the fullness of her breasts quite
as a boy grasps soap-bubbles and marvels at their
intact resistance. He could have possessed her without recovering from the thinly juvenile daze that
had exiled the inflated inanities of Purrel, the philandering stockbroker, and substituted a whirling,
diffident serf in his place.

Jessica began to feel that scarcely tangible meeting of sleep and wakefulness, which overcomes a
woman with such an imperceptible assurance that
she hardly knows what has happened until she suddenly feels the gross readjustments of a more discernible reality. Unless their sex is in the grip of
an undiscriminating starvation, most women succumb to an enraptured dream—and a despairing attempt to preserve something finely unreal that must
not be permitted to betray them too soon. Even the
most sensitive of men, at such a time, never quite
experience this buoyant cleavage from room and
garments, and their transports are at best always
more cruel and awake.

Purrel's hands had left Jessica's breast and were slowly becoming more impetuous, when pain brought her back to the music room. The frame of the piano, below the keys, was pressing into her lower spine, like an absurd remonstrance that made her mood prosaic in the passing of a second. Sex thrives upon comfort as a secondary but indispensable drug, and no woman except a callow girl or a matter-of-fact courtesan can retain her abandonment if she feels that she is being humorously maltreated. The greatest love can be turned in a thrice to the silliest of frauds by a breaking chair, or the prolonged creaking of a couch. It would almost seem as though an essential insincerity in all love were always waiting for outside mishaps to proclaim its presence.

Jessica slipped under Purrel's arms and stood up, her hands darting guiltily as she rearranged her dress, and an expression of surprised self-rebuke was on her face. The heavy, devilish resentment which some people feel just after they have emerged from ether came to her. Purrel was once more a fat nuisance of a man who had tried to redeem his dullness with a physical temerity, and she had barely saved herself from accommodating this commonplace desire. She was becoming a carnal fool and demeaning the preciousness of her body.

Purrel felt feverish and thwarted without knowing

why——she was certainly the hardest case that he had ever handled——and he opened his cigarette case to simulate self-control.

"Ted, you must go home," she said. "I want to be alone. I don't know why I let you do all these things to me. We've simply got to act differently toward each other."

An instinct within Purrel told him to walk out to the hallway for his hat and coat without saying a word. He acted largely through "hunches"—— warnings and affirmations that came from an unsurveyed part of him. When he had departed, with a mere "Good night, see you again, Jes," and Jessica was lying on the bed in her room, she felt relieved and indifferent. The entire evening became a pointless escapade that fitted into those which she had had with seven or eight other men during the past year ——she couldn't even remember the number.

After all, you allowed men to make love to you because it would have been a dreary task to carry around a body whose existence had no power in itself to affect other people. The amorous tactics of men prevented the more thoughtful parts of your life from becoming too monotonous——you couldn't paint pictures or converse seriously all of the time, and you had to titillate your sense of being alive during the intervals. Men must scarcely ever be permitted to possess you, for otherwise you lost for a time the feeling of playful erectness, and in the rare cases when you did permit them it was unwise to remember anything about it. A bit sulky and mortified, you made a more intense resolution never to yield again.

Jessica failed to see that one half of her spirit was empty and the other half richly vainglorious, and that her flirtations with life and thought served to minimize the clashes between these rival parts. One day she regarded herself as an accomplished artist and thinker, and on another day she became dejected and felt that she was merely deceiving herself before the eventual church ceremony, with its solemn mummeries of organ music and verbal pledges. Men were needed to divert the aftermaths caused by these moods, and without men she would have sunk to an open self-dislike. Her twenty-three years had given her a tangle of cynicisms and sentimentalities. The sexologists and realistic novelists whom she had read competed with the deaf anticipations within her heart and the touch of poetry fluttering through the coldness of her head, and the result was an indeterminate uproar. Life showed you so many ugly and beautiful faces that you couldn't gather them to any one individuality or meaning. Most people were indeed dressed-up animals, but you knew two or three winsome exceptions —or were they exceptions?—and they laughed at your pessimism. Again, perhaps you yourself were no better than most people in this respect, except that you avoided looking at yourself, with a sprightly cleverness. No, she was libeling herself—she wanted to express herself in paint and words, and rise far above her limbs. But for a person who had such a dominant desire, her contacts with the arms of men were remarkably numerous. Oh, it was all a hopeless, blundering mess and nothing could be gained by endlessly trying to analyze your relation to it. It was better to see different people and make every effort to like or dislike them, and play with paint on canvas because it soothed your discontents, and let the rest take care of itself.

When she had attended college, her life had been a ceaseless shifting between giddiness and contemplation. On one week she would dance or go automobile-riding every night, and on the next she would shut herself up in her dormitory room and read Nietzsche and Dostoievsky. She wanted to be adored and to be wise at the same time, and she could not determine which desire was the more sincere, and she became a coquette and a recluse with equal fervor because she wanted to give each one a chance to drive out the other. Books delighted her for two weeks at most, and the philosophical ones overtaxed her mind but made it proudly fight to hold their meanings, while the fictional ones often showed her quirks and qualms in human beings that she could never have come upon herself. Then the books began to seem an ingeniously black and white lie about life—life was never quite like these printed scenes and people, even when they were portrayed with a startling skill. The ideas of the philosophers were elaborate attempts to catch something that was too quick and simple for their nets. Life itself stood outside of the books and was more tumultuously attractive, for it was the original voice and not the interpretation. Life was a warm, blasphemous, hilarious, impossible, beckoning affair, and it asked you to return to it and desert the paper leaves.

The reaction always came suddenly. She would be sitting at the window of her room and reading when the brazen jigging of a hurdy-gurdy would rise from the street. The music, a popular song of the day—gay, crude, and sensual—would become life, reminding her that she had been neglecting it. Then she would throw the book aside and run down to the front hall and countermand the order that she had given the maids to tell every one except her father that she was "not in." And that night she went to a dance, with some handsome, blithely "kidding" youth, and liked the smothering of his breast, and felt gleefully empty and volatile, and stood in the dormitory hallway with him and allowed him to caress her to that point where "goodnight" was a sorely needed rescue. And on two, widely separated nights, while drinking from the pocket-flask of the boy beside her, as they were both seated in an automobile, she had felt something within her say: "Come on, stop being afraid of this thing," and she had yielded herself to the boy with a sense of begging curiosity that was mesmerized for a moment and then slowly cheated. Afterwards, on the drive home, she had treated each boy with a tart aloofness and had promptly forgotten about him and ignored his letters and telephone calls. He had served his purpose, and he was not attractive in other ways, and he must not be led to believe that she was an instrument of pleasure waiting for his summons, and through disregarding him she could revenge herself for the semblance of prostration that she had once given him.

Jessica differed from the other college girls in the fact that she refused to mix up her mind with her emotions, or to align herself only with one or the other. A majority of the girls were fidgeting quintessences of sex, and their thoughts were little more than a weak, reluctant lull between their "dates" with this man and that. A minority of the girls went to the other extreme and studied furiously, and had their eyes steadily turned to a career, and accompanied men only at rare times and with an air of succumbing to a dangerous luxury. Jessica played both of these games alternately and without favoritism, which made it hard for her friends and acquaintances to classify her, except certain youths who compared notes on "how far she had let them go." The distance being equal in almost all of the cases, the youths regarded her as a "teaser" but had a piqued liking for her, while the girls disliked her as a rule because she provoked their perceptions and they could not tell whether she was "regular" or not.

The fact that she was the only child of a million-aire father, and that her mother had been dead for several years, had little effect on Jessica's make-up. No mother would have succeeded in governing and subduing her in the smallest extent, and money was the least important thing in life to her, and if she had been poor she would have slighted it with the same fervor. It could bring you "spiffy," lovely clothes, but dressing was more a matter of taste and artistry, and several of the poor girls whom she knew dressed far better than the wealthy ones, be-cause the poor girls knew what to buy and what would blend into their figures and colorings. Money could bring you the best of foods, recreations, and surroundings, but if you were poor, you had but to use your wits to obtain the same things from wealthy suitors. Why on earth did girls worry so much about money? In a way it was too bad that she had so much of it, because it deprived her of the pleas-ure of procuring its equivalents through the exercise of her wits and her sex.

After graduating from college she plagued her father until he allowed her to live in the "bohemian" section of the city—in a studio of her own—where wealthy artists and their satellites resided in a fa-mously known alley. She had tired of this place, after a month, and had returned to her home. The flock of young men, who had heard that she was a millionaire's daughter, bored her with gin and worn poetry in equal parts, and usually invited her cynicism

by asking for a loan which would enable them to
paint the masterpiece or write the epoch-shattering
novel or lyric (if their creations only *had* been masterpieces—but they never were!). As for the inevitable, "red-blooded" business men, one did not
have to live in a studio to meet them, while the
Broadway captivators usually insisted on ruining the
furniture when you rejected them.

She continued to paint after returning home—
semi-futuristic landscapes, and still-lifes, and heads
that gave the shadow-crowded and almost empty
side of her the spur of "self-expression." You had
to do something that would set you apart from the
rest of the world, or else you felt stifled, and cross,
and small. You had to believe in what you were
doing, also, even though you had a sneaking fear
that it didn't amount to much, to rid yourself of the
intermittent feeling that you were just a nicely turned
figure of flesh whom some man would eventually
marry. She made her father tear down part of the
roof of the three-story house in which they lived,
and put in a sky-light, and she painted on mornings
and afternoons, during those times when the sport
of sex had become painful in its nakedness. She
still visited the "bohemian" section of the city now
and then, to hear about the latest fads in art and to
stand some artist or writer on his head and sympathize with him as he tried to court her from the
difficult position. She had no illusions concerning
the people in this region, but their deceptions were

frequently amusingly garish and not as dolorously dependable as those of the semi-society world, and one man among them might possibly be different— Kurt Salburg, an Alsatian painter. He moved with a droll listlessness, and his worldly wisdoms always seemed to be parrying with a kind of fugitively persistent idealism, and you could never decide whether he was real or unreal, and he was fairly young— just thirty—but had the paradox of mature youth in his appearance and manners. She couldn't even tell whether he was mercenary—he had painted a portrait of her and refused a large sum from her father, and then two days later had asked her to loan him one hundred dollars. Oh, he would "explode" soon and pester her with some stupid designs. Still, she might be misjudging him—there must be one exception in every consignment, and once in a while some of them were exceptionally exceptional. In the meantime she was very poor at guessing what his next sentence would be, which was a sufficient reason for seeing him.

Why couldn't he make love to her as proficiently as Purrel did—what bug started that fairy-tale about Europeans being subtle and gradual in their emotional devices? Every one that she had ever known had grabbed her as though she were a bundle waiting for his condescension, and had whispered that his love was too imperative to be denied. Salburg, Purrel, Levine, the lawyer, the boy who had written a poem to her hair . . . men . . . always more men

. . . self-confident, hairy creatures . . . brains as alike as their trousers . . . foolish to stop Purrel's hands . . . no, mustn't see him again. . . . Jessica fell asleep and passed dreamlessly out of life until her maid woke her up at 9 A.M. This was her customary hour of rising, unless she came home at an unusually late hour, in which case she would pin a note to one of the posters of her bed, instructing the maid to rouse her at noon.

Another day—teasing, slant-eyed, with unexpected interests daring you to catch them, or lukewarm, well-ordered, depressing: which would it be? Life always held out the lure of a surprising turn and reminded you that such an incident had really happened to you once every half year or so, and so you were induced to rise from the bed, although at bottom it would have been better to have remained on the bed and departed from all deceits and disappointments. But no, it was morning, and your blood ran with a fine, irresistible speed, and your emotions became softly athletic and almost hopeful. What was the day's program—two hours of painting, a luncheon of the Jason League at the Billington Hotel—how she wished that she could get out of going—and a matinee at a play in which a clergyman was seduced by a bad woman—somehow they never reversed the positions of the characters in this situation—and a visit to Salburg's studio, with the evening unarranged and problematical.

Her maid was a lean, Irish girl, with woodenish

legs and an ingeniously half-pretty face that was always placidly calculating. While she was curling Jessica's bobbed hair, Jessica eyed her with a tinge of interest. Did any thought ever wriggle behind that carefully peaceful, facial expression?

"Did you go out last night?" asked Jessica.

"Yes, ma'am, I did."

"I hope you let him do something to you," said Jessica.

"Why, no indeed, I never let men take liberties with me!"

"Tell me another one, Kathleen, I like to hear you."

"Well, it doesn't pay to give in to a man unless he's after marrying you," said Kathleen. "I was foolish once, but I won't be again."

"You were happy once, you mean, and you got angry because it didn't last, and then you decided to wait till you found one that was guaranteed to hang around. That's probably it."

"I really don't know just what you mean," answered Kathleen.

"You'd better take your thrills as they come— none of them will ever stay more than a month anyway, and marriage doesn't change it any."

"I just don't think you're right, Miss Jessica. There's nothing better than having a home of your own and a decent, good-looking man to take care of you. Of course, you won't be crazy about him forever, but then everybody's got to settle down some time."

"Tra-la-la, I've read that somewhere, haven't I? I'll curl the rest of it myself, Kathleen. Get that chiffon thing out and the blue smock I bought last week."

Kathleen felt resentful as she walked away, and she longed to tell Jessica "a thing or two." These rich girls—always poking a finger into your private affairs and trying to show you how wise they were! Jessica probably acted bad with a lot of men—she didn't get in at three in the morning for nothing—and thought that every other girl was like her. Oh, they didn't believe in marrying, did they? Well, if she, Kathleen, had Jessica's money, maybe she wouldn't be so interested in marriage either. It was really a shame the way Jessica carried on—what on earth made her father stand for it? Two-thirds of Kathleen's irritation was caused by the fact that a husky truck-driver had subdued her on the previous evening and she felt that Jessica suspected what had happened without knowing who the man was. Kathleen was continually uttering righteous words and submitting to any man who was young, with regular features, and willing to spend money freely, and with each submission her words grew fiercer and more moral, partly because the words almost made her forget what had happened and partly because she always resolved never to submit again and always felt a bit of shame afterwards. But the next automobile pick-up, or second-rate cabaret party, found her weakly and futilely resisting another man. There was always something to drink and it gave her a hazy, conquering, don't-care feeling and threw out all of the words and resolutions as though they were so much excess baggage that she was tired of carrying around. She belonged to a prudishly dissembling, half-courtesan class whose members are abundantly strewn among the working girls of a city, and who toil each day to keep up a pitiful deception which they hope will lead to a prosperous or endurable marriage.

When Jessica came down to the breakfast table her father and aunt were fiddling with their coffee, in the manner that people have when their thoughts are erratically interfering with the dwindling urge of food. Cloyd Maringold was a half-bald, fat-faced man whose fifty years had brought him inner lines and an outward smoothness. Certain men have the skins of striplings, even though they are nearing the end of middle age, because they were canny enough to shelve their dissipations between long periods of repentance, and because no man or woman ever mattered enough to them to bring the wrinkles of any great grief, and because they began to smile for business reasons at an early age and gradually grew into the smile, relying upon humor to deepen and protect the natural blindness of their minds. Maringold had a little black hair on the back of his head, and a nose that was a caricature of Jessica's.

tilting steeply out above the nostrils, and thick, closed lips, and eyes that were shrewd but strove to be merry. Somehow, you saw a feeble cruelty on his face, toned down by years of grinning but still functioning beneath the obsession of good-nature which he had found to be so materially profitable. In a crisis he could knife a man without hesitation, but it was his specialty to make the victim laugh with him over the lack of pain involved, and in this process Maringold himself was aided in believing that his action had been justified. Men liked him because he knew how to be sufficiently generous in small matters to make these men lenient toward his larger raids. In the general opinion he was a hard business man but amazingly decent in spite of that fact. A blending of luck and intuitive cunning in problems which his head alone could never have solved had brought him his millions, while his smile had added the finishing touches.

He was of English blood, though born in America, and had married in London while visiting his relatives during his youth. His wife had been a frail, unworldly, meek girl from the English middle class, with faint literary aspirations and an indecisive mind. She had married him because he was not less presentable than other men whom she knew and seemed to have a kindly steadiness that promised her peace if not happiness. In addition, she had wanted to leave her unsympathetic parents and had visualized living in America as a strange, pleasantly risky adventure. She had died shortly after giving birth to Jessica and he had not married again because he had been unfaithful to his wife and did not wish to return to a second strain upon his conscience. The girls and women whom he desired physically, and whose speech was entertaining, did not have the breeding and respectability which he considered essential for a wife, and though he often wavered because he wanted a son to carry his name on, he became gradually enamored with the sexual promiscuity that could be captured without reproaches and falsehood. You couldn't devour your cake without leaving tell-tale crumbs behind, and it was better to shield the feast with an irresponsible privacy. He was careful to keep his amours hidden and to stage them only with unattached, half-respectable women, to whom his money and strong body were irresistible.

Now, at fifty, his indiscretions had petered out to very occasional visits to the apartments of actresses and chorus girls, but he never allowed himself to be seen in public with them and refrained from writing any letters that might afterwards prove to be expensive. He regarded Jessica as an improved version of her mother—with a greater health and prettiness that were wedded to the delicacies and graces left by the dead woman (men who failed to love their wives in life often deify them in death because the after-worship soothes their self-accusations and demands no sacrifice). He considered Jessica to be unbalanced and willful, and her artistic aims were perplexing follies to him, but he consented to all of her wishes and made no effort to order her life because her mental swiftness overawed him and convinced him that she could take care of herself. Any one who could get the best of his girl would have to be an inhumanly sharp actor indeed! Besides, no child of his could possibly be lacking in the saving, practical virtues that had lifted him to affluence.

Beneath these reasons spoken to himself, there were other ones. He knew that he was not the kindly, conventional, and moral person that the world thought him to be, and this knowledge darkened his spirit sometimes and made him long for a greater balm than the Episcopalian church which he often attended. His acquiescent affection for Jessica was an outlet for the few kinder impulses in his life which he had killed while seeming to cherish them, and the boon of her existence made them strong in their own belief and silenced his self-reproaches. As for the conventional and moral part of it, his rôle of respectable and devoted father was needed to counterbalance his midnight pranks with women, and he looked upon Jessica's own escapades as no more than a harmless exuberance. Since he felt that his own sensual intensities might have been transferred to her, he was not certain as to whether she was still a virgin, but so far she had entered into no discernible entanglements with men and always seemed to keep five or six of them hopping to her tune (a sign of wary coquetry, if not absolute chastity). Evidently she could be relied upon not to lose her head (a Maringold trait). Eventually, she would marry, but there was no reason for haste. If a girl married in her late twenties, or even at thirty, she was far more liable to make a sober and responsible choice, with her blood cooled down and her judgment more prosaic by that time.

Jessica's aunt on her mother's side, Roberta Swinson, was a washed-out, submissive woman of forty-five. Her scant, brown hair was as apparent and straightly bound as her mind, and she had a shrunken face, with a long nose, forever blinking, weakly blue eyes, and thinly troubled lips. She had accepted Maringold's invitation to come to America and take care of Jessica after the mother's death, and she looked upon Jessica as a more aggressive image of the sister whom she had never liked. Jessica's mother had been a freakish, softly insincere creature in Roberta's opinion, and Jessica had taken after her. Robert had raised Jessica with much care and many semblances of affection, secretly hoping that it would bring her a proposal of marriage from Maringold, and when the years had passed without this proposal she had continued these semblances from the momentum of habit and because she was materially dependent upon him. To avoid gossip he had first installed Jessica and Roberta in a separate household and had lived at his club, but after the years had increased his wealth he had purchased the Fifth Avenue house in which they were all residing. Roberta's chief interests now were social functions, at which she could sit with other women and flay the scandals of the day, and the smaller ones in her own set; and theaters, where she could secretly sneer at all of the characters who were not proper while admiring them even more secretly; and suggestive novels which she read surreptitiously. All of her life had resolved to a half-hearted duel between dying sex and the platitudes springing from a luxurious existence. In her opinion she was a woman who had escaped from the atrocious snares of what people called love—the two "affairs" of her youth had become the faintest of goblins—and had sensibly earned the security and ease which she would never have gained had she not stilled the foolishness once within her heart. Such women, who have never lived, must change their vision of life to avoid the fact that most of them have perished, and must change it so imperceptibly and thoroughly that they reach a condition of "benevolent" abdication, with every figment of self-perception destroyed.

Sitting at the breakfast table, Maringold greeted his daughter warmly, while Roberta was more composed. Jessica liked her father because she suspected that he was and had been a dexterous sinner, and because his solicitude and generosity made her own affection almost compulsory, but she had no respect for him. She felt that his mind had as much penetration as that of a chimpanzee, and that he was æsthetically void, and she knew about the legal

skirmishes with dishonesty which he frequently carried out in his business. He was a fraud, of course,
but a mild and often repentant one, and you simply
had to be lenient to your own father—fathers were
not appropriate subjects for dissection and did not
require a close inspection unless they persisted in
bothering your habits.

"I bought you the tubes of paint you wanted,"
said Maringold. "You'll find them up in the studio.
I felt silly asking for them. The clerk must have
thought I looked very peculiar for an artist-chap."

"Oh, artists often look much worse than you do,
father. Don't take it to heart. He—or was it a
she?—probably thought you were some sort of
commercial one—entirely too prosperous."

"Jes-si-ca, you might be more respectful to your
father," said Roberta.

"Now that's exactly what I don't want," said
Maringold. "I remember, when I was first traveling
out West to look over the ranch I had, how the cow-
boys used to pummel each other around. You'd
think they were fighting each other, I swear, and yet
they were really the best of friends. It was just
their way of liking each other, that's all. Jessie
has the same idea."

"You do give me the loveliest excuses, father,"
Jessica said. "They're much better than any I could
think up."

"Well, you need them, Jessie," said Roberta.
"You're positively impudent at times, and I know

that you don't mean anything by it, but you might control it more just the same."

"Auntie, it occurs to me that we've discussed this thing for a hundred breakfasts," Jessica answered. "We might be a little more original, don't you think?"

"I'm never quarreling, I'm sure," said Roberta. "I simply have my own ideas and I like to express them."

Jessica felt like asking Roberta what idea she had ever meant to express, but she didn't. She saw all of the faded meanness and censored burials in Roberta and idly pitied her.

"I'll have to ask you for another three hundred, father," said Jessica.

"And four hundred last week. You might as well take it all at once—it would be more convenient—" said Maringold amiably, as he drew out his check book.

Roberta always clung to her rôle of placid objector, for she felt it her duty to inject some equilibrium into these jauntily extravagant people.

"Haven't you been spending rather freely this week?" she asked of Jessica. "I don't object, of course, but you know when I drop in at the Charity Bureau sometimes and see the per-fect-ly wretched cases there, I often think it's really not fair for the rest of us to be so careless about money."

"Well, Auntie, I came into a cruel world and I don't feel like crusading against it," said Jessica.

"Nobody would need any charity if everybody weren't innately selfish, and I don't know just how much you help people by throwing figurative pennies at them once in a while. It might be better to give them everything or nothing, I think."

"That sounds just a little, well, socialistic to me," Roberta answered. "I'm really surprised at you, Jessie. All of us ought to do our share toward helping the misery in the world but it would be simply ridiculous to give people more than they need."

"Oh, Jessie likes to be cynical, and it doesn't hurt her any," said Maringold. "There is something, of course, in charity undermining a person's respect, but that doesn't happen unless you give him money when he's able to take care of himself. Besides, Roberta, you can never understand that the younger generation likes to appear very bold and radical but doesn't believe in what it's talking about. You take everything they say so seriously."

"Will I ever grow up to be wonderful and wise, like you, father," said Jessica. "It worries me so much I can't sleep at night."

"I think you must have been worried about something else last night," her father answered, unruffled.

(No child ever confessed its actual respect for a father unless it was out of its mind, and whatever radical ideas Jessica had must be affected ones since they never intruded upon the trends of her life.)

"I heard you tripping up the stairs after one," he went on. "Ted Purrel was here, I suppose."

"And everything was so remarkably quiet," said Roberta. "I didn't hear you banging on the piano, as usual."

"What a terrible insinuation," answered Jessica, lightly. "If I protested too much about it, it would sound guilty, so I won't."

"You could pick out several men worse than Purrel," Marginold said. "He's rated at over half a million on the Street, and besides, he seems to be a good-looking, upstanding kind of a man."

"Yes, I could, and I probably will," answered Jessica, blithely, as they all rose from the table.

She spent the next two hours in her studio, where she worked on a small painting of what appeared to be two lavender pineapples placed on each side of a slender, black and white vase, all of the articles standing on a dark red table that seemed about to fall to the cerise floor. Her adoration of color came from the taut, negroid touch in her nature—from the childlike, high-pitched sensuality which thrust aside her sophistications at unexpected moments. She painted because it was an outlet through which she could ridicule the remainder of her life and banish all of the formalities, and coverings, and dodgings with which her days were full. Futuristic painting, which offers a delectable freedom to the beginner, gave her a chance to knock topsy-turvy the world that she moved in, and disport with angles, and leers, and explosions. This was not insincere on her part because she needed to express certain emotions that were too boisterous to fit into sexual affairs and too impertinent to be voiced to other people. She had a moderate talent for painting and had participated in a few exhibits under an assumed name, from the fear that otherwise her work might be accepted solely because of her wealth and social position.

When noon came she donned a dark green, duvetyn gown, and a chipper, gray hat of the latest bell-shaped style, and drove down to the Billington Hotel in her runabout. The social set in which her family mingled stood midway between the upper and lower portions of the city's society realm. Since her father's wealth had not been inherited and had been acquired during the past fifteen years, she was not eligible to mix with the "best families," and they rarely invited her to their functions, except as an afterthought, although she was acquainted with many of their daughters and sons. On the other hand, her crowd was not one of those "rich-over-night" gangs that spring up in American metropoles and bunglingly emulate the trappings and practices of society "leaders," or become risque and ribald, as a daring advertisement of their prosperity. Her family was among those residing just inside the borders of the higher social world—bands of approved apprentices—indulgently regarded by the kings and queens and sometimes added to the court festivities as a quiet test of their fitness and credentials. These bands made no effort to be ostentatious, but soberly sought to prove their worth in the battle for a more assured social position, although the younger members frequently transgressed in matters of taste and exuberance and had to be admonished by their elders. These groups made at least a brave attempt to be cultured and correct, and their next generation, if it remained in the city, would begin to graduate to the topmost social plane. Maringold owned a summer home in a fashionable Long Island colony, had his box at the opera, belonged to the "right" golf and yachting clubs, and had managed, three years previous, to get his name into one of the legitimate Blue Books.

When Jessica arrived at a private banquet hall of the Billington Hotel the débutantes and younger veterans were already eating. Often people satirize themselves much more effectively than any one else could and it becomes pointless to continue the destruction, unless you can do it very whimsically, or with the lightest of rapiers and shoulder shrugs, and this was Jessica's thought as she looked at the faces around her. That she was in some respect not different from the owners of these faces did not occur to her. She had an intelligence that could see the faults and poses of people but failed to see that she herself was deliberately reiterating them because it pleased the lazier and more conforming side of her. An individual often imagines that he is a secret bystander to those around him without discerning that he is also watching much the same qualities within himself. Jessica's excuse often repeated to herself, for mingling with these girls, was that they were just as diverting as any other group would be so it didn't matter much, although sometimes a rush of boredom would cause her to shun them for a month or so. She teetered back and forth between the "art" and social worlds without knowing that she was escaping from different parts within herself.

She sat at a table between two friends, Gloria Seabrook and Ethel Daniels. Gloria was a tall, slender girl with a small, plump face. She was flawlessly pretty, with large, black eyes, a straight nose, bow-shaped lips, and a pale, brown skin. She happened to be passing through an Oriental craze and wore a softly gaudy, batique dress, stamped with Egyptian hieroglyphics, a white turban, long earrings of green jade, and broad gold bands around her bare arms. She had refused to bob her hair because you never knew when you would want it back again and wigs were impossible. She had lived twenty-one years and they had given her a furore of sophistications and naïvetés. She knew much about sex and its devices and perversions, but little about life and the people in it: she could rattle off phrases on every subject, from politics to poetry, and the phrases were smartly turned and sometimes her own, but if you had pinned her down you would have run across astonishingly ignorant beliefs. She thought that most of the world was honest, and kind, and happy, except a small part of it which was regularly locked up in jails and asylums so that it couldn't harm the other part.   Even the people who lived in slums were happy in their own unambitious, dirty way, and when they were very destitute they received the charity of good-hearted people.   The only really disturbing factor was sex—it made men run away with other men's wives, and women with other women's husbands, and it induced girls to ruin themselves for the sake of good-looking boys, and it made old men act in a silly way toward young enchantresses.   You had to keep a cool head in this sex problem and stop yourself from falling in love with any man who was not wealthy and well-born, although, of course, you could play around with other men and let them flatter you and caress you in any way that would not produce dangerous consequences.

Gloria's friend, Ethel Daniels, looked on Gloria as a clever, unscrupulous baby who should have been spanked now and then for her own good.   Ethel considered herself to be a practical, finely balanced person who knew that dreams of any kind were both flimsy and harmful and that it was better to take what you could get when you were able to get it, and make the best of it.   It was a woman's duty to look as beautiful as she could, and take an interest in the financial affairs of her family so that she would be capable of running them some day, and marry a sober man of her own crowd and have two children, and enjoy herself sensually in ways that were moderate and properly robed, and fulfill her responsibilities toward life by engaging in some kind of charitable and civic work now and then. Cocktails and kisses were not improper if you held them to a judicious minimum. You had to have emotions—there was no way out of it—but there were so many harmless methods of gratifying them, such as amateur theatricals, dancing, naughty plays, etc. Ethel was short and pale, with much blonde hair and a bluntly handsome face. Only reducing exercises kept her from being stout and she had a compulsory love for athletic games. She prattled to Jessica on the subject of tennis.

"Jes', why don't you come out to Beaver Hills?" she asked. "We have the loveliest courts there, and all the experts visit us. I played a game with Will Bowman the other day. He's number four on the ranking list, you know."

"He's number six hundred and forty-four on my ranking list," said Jessica, indifferently.

"Why will you cling to that pose," said Ethel, exasperated. "You know perfectly well that you don't really care for those queer artists that you run around with. They give you a thrill with all of their talk and eccentricities, I know, but you'd be absolutely bored if you had to live with one of them a single week. They never wear beyond a night. They're not real, wholesome men, and you know it as well as I do."

"They're certainly not," answered Jessica, plac-idly, "and that's why I like them. You see, it doesn't really matter to you, dear, whether a man says anything to you or not as long as he's good-looking and pleasant, but you mustn't expect every one else to be the same."

"Jes', you're the only person I know who can make me feel like swearing out loud," said Ethel. "Your idea of a man is simply gorgeous. Some one who tells you about your so-oul, and all of the hidden desires you've got, and what a terrible mess life is, and don't you think that most people are hor-ri-bly stupid. And all of the time he's wondering how long he ought to wait before he puts his arms around you."

"Well, even that would be an improvement on men who don't wonder so much," said Jessica. "It's all according to your taste, dear. If you're only interested in dancing around and playing at being alive you won't care to hear a man who tells you about the influence of the primitives on modern art. Whenever a man starts to talk about your soul or your sex it's never interesting or uninteresting in it-self—it all depends on whether he has anything new to say. Most of them haven't, but there's no rule about it."

"I think Jes' is right," said Gloria. "Mother often has artists and writers up to the house and I love to listen to them. They say such strange things and they're so charmingly insolent about it. Of

course, you couldn't seriously fall in love with them
—Ethel's right there—but it's ridiculous to meet the
same kind of people all the time. I'd talk to a truck-
driver if I thought I could get away with it."

"You're both utterly impossible," said Ethel.
"You imagine you're very daring and extreme and
you're nothing of the kind. I'd like to bet that in
ten years from now you'll be fussing over your babies
and telling the cook what to have for dinner."

"Babies," exclaimed Gloria. "I'm never, never
going to have them. They make you look like fifty
when you're just beginning to live. I don't care
whether it's selfish or not, but I'm going to adopt
some and treat them just as though they were my
own, and if my husband doesn't like it he can get a
divorce. I never could see why every woman on
earth must have children, whether she wants to or
not. If one woman has seven or eight of them it
certainly ought to make up for another woman having none at all."

"That's quite logical, though of course you won't
be fulfilling your duty to the race, whatever that is,"
said Jessica, lightly.

"It's a good thing that the world isn't depending
on girls like you two," answered Ethel. "Everything
would go to a smash in a jiffy, otherwise. Besides,
I can't understand a woman who hasn't any mother-
love in her—there must be something fundamentally
wrong with her spirit."

"I know that I'm a terrible and imperfect creature

and I'm absolutely conscience stricken about it," said Jessica, "but it doesn't seem to do me any good. The more conscience stricken I become the worse I get. Will you sympathize with me, Ethel, if I come to a bad end?"

Gloria laughed and Ethel said something about determinedly insincere people. The chairman of the luncheon, a vivacious girl with a pink face that was always barely restraining itself from becoming hoydenish and ill-bred, made a speech about plans for the coming street affair that was to be held by the Jason League. There would be fortune-telling booths and booths for the sale of knickknacks and artcraft stuff, and a dancing pavilion, and the proceeds would go to a home for elderly cripples. The girls at the tables were assigned their duties at the fair, and they babbled over the delightful pact between benevolence and fox-trots. Jessica was given the task of making quick sketches of people at ten dollars apiece and accepted it because it would be a jocund opportunity to inject a slight element of caricature into drawings that would seem to be innocent at a first glance.

She managed to excuse herself, and hurried to the matinee with Gloria, where they saw a play about a minister and a courtesan marooned on a tropical island. The minister resisted the wiles of the courtesan and strove to reform her, but just as he was on the verge of converting her, he collapsed beneath the strain and returned to his manhood. This startling descent disillusioned the courtesan and she tottered forth, once more bitterly convinced that all men resembled each other, that virtue was an abundance of fine-sounding words employed to save the lust of men from becoming naked and embarrassed, and that religion was not observed by those who preached it.   Jessica saw the absurdity of this characterization and climax—in seven cases out of ten the woman would have patted the clergyman on the back afterwards and congratulated him upon his murder of hypocrisy, without being deeply moved, and in the eighth case she would have loved him and wept to hold his affections, and in the ninth case she would have quietly shunned him as a person too falsely solemn and inane for her contempt, and in the tenth case her reactions would have been more poetic and helter-skelter.   Yet, Jessica was engrossed by the play because its falsehoods were skillfully and feverishly assembled and glossed over, and because the actors were talented enough to rescue their artificial lines with vocal inflections and well-placed gestures that made them seem real for the moment. The trick of all successful realistic plays is to give the characters the vernacular that they would use in actual life, and all of the uppermost foibles in conduct and appearance that people of their kind would have, while at the same time assigning these people theatrical, high-pitched, and preposterous motives and plots.

These thoughts, in a modified form, flitted through

Jessica's head during the intervals between the acts, but when the curtain parted again she felt almost persuaded that she was watching and listening to a real minister and courtesan. This contradiction often extended to the rest of her life—the ability to view a situation judicially when she was removed from it, and to become an easy victim when she was experiencing it. Gloria, on the other hand, believed that the play was both true and mar-vel-ous. The minister was a handsome, noble man and the abominable woman had taken advantage of him and he wasn't really to blame, and such women deserved to be punished. What a frightful world this would be if every one thought only of sex, and why did people let it hurt them so much? In her reactions there was a tinge of youthful spite against women who dared to do things that were appealing but frightening to her, and she sided with the man in the play because he was part of the appeal itself.

After the matinée, Jessica and Gloria parted, and Jessica drove to Salburg's studio. Salburg was a stocky man of medium height, with a shock of blond hair that often dropped over his high forehead, and a shaved, saurian face. Looking at his sluggish face, you felt that, like a crocodile, it could release the quickest words and motives if its prey happened to be within reach. He had a nose steeply indented near the top, which gave him a Semitic twist although he was in reality a Gentile, and his lips were thick and forever parted, and his gray eyes were almost closed and yet gave a sense of looking at you through their lids. Like many painters—even foremost ones —he had an æsthetic sureness that had nothing to do with his mind, and mentally he was little more than a child repeating the lessons of its instructors when not rebelling against them. Yet, he had mastered the ability of appearing in conversation to be far wiser than he actually was, by the use of epigrams whose meanings he was not certain of himself. He had an instinct for knowing what was the "right" and "wrong" thing to say and he could make a seemingly penetrating remark without knowing why he had said it, or whether he believed it. There was a Prussian element in his outlook on women and they were to him fickle, posing, and inferior creatures of flesh, whose chief value was a physical one which tested your powers as a romantic and unusual liar. You made every possible kind of overture and dissembling and protest to them until you had absolutely possessed them, after which you became more open and brutal, and showed them what their place was.

Jessica's attraction to him was a physical one made more intense by the fact that she had gracefully repulsed most of his overtures. To be sure, she had a swift mind and a light sense of humor, but these were incidentals adding a bit more of charm. If she had been a stumbling-tongued peasant girl, with the same face and figure, he would have pursued her just as ardently. However, he did sense in her an unusually wary and formidable pride, and this made him anticipate a victory over her with more satisfaction, since it would sweeten his general feeling of mastery over women.

When he greeted her with a bow and raised her hand to his lips, she smiled—they did it so well and it meant absolutely nothing to them. He had been painting and he removed his stained smock and donned a black velvet coat before he sat beside her. The studio was a high, large place, cluttered with odds and ends—a Turkish scimitar, some primitive sculpture reproductions in bronze and terra-cotta, framed canvases of his own in the post-impression-istic manner, Japanese prints, batiques, fencing foils, huge pipes, etc. The furniture was plain wood brightly painted over, and a low couch covered with brown cloth stood in a corner. In his belief, the place that you worked in needed to be a conglom-eration of moods and articles instead of holding one, central note which might irritate you half of the time.

"What have you been doing, Liebchen?" he asked.

"Liebchen? Have you been possessing me in my sleep, Kurt, or is this your way of commencing?"

"You would not have noticed the word if you had not been thinking of such a possibility," he answered, in his distinctly syllabled English that always seemed to be afraid of making a mis-step.

"And if I hadn't noticed it I'd be guilty of accepting its inference," said Jessica. "You're determined not to let me escape, aren't you?"

"I have discovered that women are never conscious of what a man is saying unless they desire to hear it, or—well—unless it is painfully boring to them," he responded. "I do not imagine that I have been wearying you, so . . ."

"So, on the other hand, I must be longing for you," said Jessica. "Of course, I couldn't possibly be just mildly interested in what you're saying!"

"You might think that you were," he replied. "Emotions stir within us and take their time about making themselves known to us. One can be in love with another person for months without realizing it, and then suddenly an accidental silence, or a stray word—some little thing—can change the whole situation. Once I met a woman for six months, here and there and everywhere, and we gave each other nothing but the most casual sarcasms, and our eyes were always elsewhere. Then, one night, I happened to meet her on the street, and I was about to pass on after a few, empty words, when a sudden rainstorm drove both of us into a doorway. It came down like a deluge, without warning, and we had to run for shelter. Our shoulders touched as we stood in the doorway, and all at once we began to tremble. She grasped my hand, quickly, and we turned and looked at each other as though we had never met before. We had been lying to each other

for months and months without the slightest knowledge of it."

"Am I expected to be startled about this?" asked
Jessica. "You touched in the doorway, the dear,
undreamt-of doorway, and then it occurred to both
of you that you were a man and woman and probably had nothing to do for the evening. It was the
hundredth doorway for each of you, and you took a
good look at each other for the first time and decided that you might be much homelier. I wouldn't
be surprised, too, if both of you had been turned
down by some other man or woman, and you wanted
to show how little it meant to you. That's usually
the first reaction."

"Sometimes we are cynical because it saves us the
trouble of finding more difficult explanations," he
answered. "You cannot always belittle emotions by
telling them that they have been sordid and ordinary.
If you persist in doing that, then you are suggesting
that ordinary feelings are the only ones that you are
capable of having."

"You're right," she said. "When I'm not painting, or thinking things out, my emotions are very
commonplace. So are yours. The feelings that
people have for each other are very usual at bottom.
The main reason that we talk to each other, Kurt, is
to make them seem less usual and much more varied
than they are. Otherwise, we'd instantly fall into
each other's arms, and have it over with, and leave
each other."

Her vanity always refused to fall into his snares, and this disconcerted him, but her last words had suggested a simple possibility (the one among many that he might have overlooked).

"I don't agree with you, but perhaps you can convince me that we are foolish in not beginning now," he replied, lightly, placing a hand upon her bare arm.

She disengaged it and smiled.

"Now, little boy, you'll get your kisses, but you've got to go on talking for a while," she said. "Just imagine that you're paying for them and pretending not to pay, which is what most conversations between men and women amount to. You'll notice that I said most, Kurt. Perhaps you can prove to me that you're an exception."

He made a movement of great indifference.

"What are you—a merchant in disguise?" he asked. "Nothing has any value unless it does not have to be purchased. Now you make me sorry that I touched you, since it was a new dream to me and an old transaction to you."

"I'll remain silent while you get over your disillusionment," she answered. "If it really was a dream to you, you'll keep on trying to make me believe it. I'm not worrying about that."

"You are weary of yourself today," he said. "What has happened to you?"

"Nothing that could make me less weary," she replied, liking the imputation of tired superiority which he thrust upon her.

This was one of her weakest qualities—this craving for a high perch from which she could languidly and accurately survey a more active world—and he took care to encourage it with his words.

"This world of ours tires you out in spite of all your prides and impudences," he said. "I am not always over-interested in it myself It shrieks, and whispers, and rushes about to hide its stupidity, and when you ask it for an understanding, what does it give you?—a dollar bill!

"You are divinely optimistic," she responded. "Since when has money been raining upon you? And, by the way, when is your next exhibition coming off?"

"At the end of April," he replied. "The critics will hand me their old comedy—I am not extreme enough for some of them and too extreme for others. They want you to paint according to their own ideas, which makes you regret that you are one man and not sixteen."

"You always rave against critics but you'd be more indifferent to them if you weren't afraid of their attacks," she said. "We don't like to see our weak spots exposed and exaggerated, that's all."

"Yes, I might be afraid if I were in Europe," he answered. "You have no critics here—you have salesmen, agents for galleries, sheep, charlatans,

schoolboys, and shouters for one small gang or another, but no critics!"

She had touched a sore part of his egotism and he
was sincerely enraged. Twilight had come, and he
lit an electric lamp. He remembered that he had
tried every device to capture her except a direct attack. He walked up to her as she sat on the couch
and forced her to a prone position with the abrupt-
ness of his onslaught. She placed her hands around
his neck and began to choke him, and he could not
pry them away since he was crushing her arms
against his breast. He arose at last, puffing and
vexed, while she straightened her dress and looked
at him with a reflective disdain. Then she approached him and rested a hand on his arm.

"I'm not going to see you again if you do this
once more," she said. "I don't want to be dramatic
and silly about it but you must understand that I
am not Anna, the housemaid, who has come to clean
your studio. You can't throw me around whenever
the whim comes to you. I'm beginning to think that
there's only one reason for your caring to see me."

He realized that he would have to strain his ut-
most to redeem the blunder. This girl desired a
slow and patient advance and her vanity was enormous but immune to most entreaties. It demanded an
ever-increasing subtlety in your approaches, and
when it was finally charmed by the incessant finesse
of your pleadings, it would submit to you. Well, she

was worthy of your struggles—if only for the revenge that you could obtain afterwards.

"It never helps any to tell a woman that you are sorry," he replied. "If you do, she knows that you must be either a liar or an imbecile. We are not children, Jessica. I do not care for your body alone, but I am not a eunuch. I am in love with you and you are still not in love with me. We will have to let it go at that."

He had sensed that an unassuming simplicity was his only possible rescue. She felt that she had been over-harsh and a little prudish to him. After all, men and women couldn't always treat each other as though they were talkative spirits.

"Kurt, I don't want to act like a schoolgirl," she said, "but you forced it upon me. You can't hurl yourself at me and expect me to be meek and give in to you. I can't love any man who isn't spontaneous and delicate at the same time. That's the way I'm made. I'll let you kiss me, Kurt, if you still want to."

He pressed his arms around her shoulders and kissed her lips and her cheeks just under the eyes. The contacts unsteadied him and he felt unbearably tantalized. Obscene designs rose in his head and taunted him, despairingly, because he could not achieve them. But such imaginings are more successful when the woman is absent. Jessica's presence and the garmented touch of her made them an un-

necessary irritant. For a time he was on the verge
of another rough attack, but he desisted because he
felt certain that she would adhere to her threat
never to see him again. Her pride craved for the
illusion of a poetic and semi-spiritual suitor.

Damn these wealthy, capricious girls, with their
idiotic blending of cynicism, and an idealism pilfered
from a few Anglo-Saxon writers! When they were
not physically beautiful you could play them with a
cool head and rely upon their latent eagerness, but
Jessica was luring, and extremely aware of it. Perhaps if he proceeded with a despairingly inspired
skill he might still be victorious before she departed
from the studio.

His hands began to wander aimlessly, with an
imperceptible gentleness, and he whispered poetic
lines and changed the originals sufficiently to make
them unforced and impromptu, and he protested
against the torture that she was inflicting upon him,
as though he did not expect her to relent but was
giving her an opportunity to amaze him. She felt
amused, compassionate, and distrustful, and the
three emotions followed each other in such a rapid
succession that they were almost synchronized.
These men—why did everything rest upon the at-
tainment of one hour with them? They were always frantic babies when they dropped their poses,
weeping for a star and outraged when they failed

instantly to get it. Her nerves were asking her to
assent to him, but an imp within her told her to do
nothing of the kind. Let him suffer for a while—if
he really was suffering—for it would only be a test
of his sincerity. She would show him that she was
different from other women who might have immediately responded to his begging. He would
have to feel that she was exclusive and impossible
to attain, and when he seemed to believe that, then
she might give herself to him.

When his hands had passed beyond the point
where love-making remains conventional, she slipped
out of his arms.

"No, Kurt, you've got to behave yourself," she
said. "Don't act as though this were the last time
you were going to see me."

He resigned himself to defeat for that night and
became loudly amiable to cover up his anger.

On the following night she received Sydney
Levine at her home. Levine was a Jew who looked
much older than his thirty-five years. His lean,
swarthy face had been drawn together by a con-
centration upon prosaic details and worries, and its
customary expression was one of skeptical inquiry.
His high cheek-bones, broad, irregular nose, deeply
placed eyes, and thin lips, that were widely twisted
into each other, gave him the guise of a studious
hawk. He had blackish-brown hair and a head that
was a bit too large for his tall body. He was void
of imagination but he had a mind that could tabulate

facts and conditions with a sleight-of-hand swiftness, and he knew how to wheedle and impress the men with whom he dealt. He was one of the most successful criminal lawyers in the city, and he had actually fought his way up from the position of a humble law clerk in the space of ten years. This was due to a trait which is peculiarly Jewish—the ability to be aggressive and conciliating without making either quality unpleasantly conspicuous—and to his brain, which was mediocre but more briskly and painstakingly so than most of those around him, and to the fact that he could remain dispassionate in the face of insults and invectives. He was known as one of the few criminal lawyers who did not wind up their cases with perfervid bursts of oratory. His forte was to address the jury in a modest, confidential style, as though the twelve men had already been impressed by the same conclusions and did not need to be carried by storm. He might have been informally chatting with the jury over a restaurant table about things which they had both deduced, and with a slowly gracious incision he thrust his facts and theories upon them. When he faced an elocutionary lawyer it was a collision between hectic sentiment and suave persuasion, and the persuasion usually won because Levine knew how to extract and coddle the much-prized "common-sense" of his auditors. He carried this virtue into his personal life and was popular among gentiles in spite of his Semitic blood. The few enemies he had were people whom he had

outwitted or people who distrusted him because he
never joked and never showed an earthly heartiness.
He was not a member of Jessica's social ring and she
had been introduced to him in a tea room in the
"bohemian" section of the city.   Her father had objected to Jessica's receptions of Levine at the house,
but in a half-hearted way—the man was prominent,
brainy, and well-to-do, and you had to be grudgingly
democratic when confronted by such a trio of attain-
ments. Of course, if his daughter displayed any sign
of desiring to marry this man he would implacably
oppose her——he certainly didn't want to have partly
Jewish grandchildren—but until then he was helpless.

Jessica was not quite sure whether she liked or disliked Levine. He had a cool, tired, meticulous way
of speaking to her, and he seemed to be without emotions, except the transiently light ones that spring
from a conversation between two people, yet there
were rare times when his voice seemed to tighten for
a second, or when his hand drew itself to a fist as
his passionless voice went on.   One could never be
certain of human beings. Levine piqued her sex
because, during the months that she had known him,
he had never attempted anything more than a prolonged holding of hands before their farewells. This
meant that he was either inhumanly fox-like or immersed in the most fatherly of friendships, and each
evening with him advanced one or the other of these
answers. Probably, he would seek to embrace her

some night and tell her how his friendship had "suddenly" switched to the most permanent of loves.
Did men ever desert these extremes of lengthy
caution and hasty presumption? When did their
emotions unfold with a steady, slow, and natural
rhythm, rising to a wildness that you could believe
in because it was neither a common, darting lust nor
the abrupt shedding of irksome garments? All that
remained of her youthful ideals prompted these
questions within her. She was not yet willing to
admit that love could never be anything except a
fleeting, physical manifestation, made distinctive at
its best by the assisting wiles of imagination and
mental graces, but always at bottom a physical obsession that slowly or quickly subsided to pretense.
Her cynicism said that men and women fumbled for
each other's flesh and then eventually drew apart,
but such a cynicism in almost every girl of twenty-
three, down to prostitutes and gold-diggers, is an
acquired protection and not an innate removal from
life.

Jessica had continued to see Levine every week
because he was still unsolved enough to dare her
penetration. As he sat beside her now she felt an
impulse to become girlishly coquettish.

"Were you ever in love, Syd?" she asked.

"Perhaps I've been too busy trying to escape from
that word," said Levine. "I get it on all sides every
day. The pretty lady loved the man too much to
give him up so she simply had to shoot him. The

man loved his wife and killed the reptile who had stolen her from him. The cashier stole ten thousand and ran away with his beloved one. The rich gentleman loved the girl and jilted her, whereupon she turned her affections to his pocketbook and sued him. The girl had a bad habit of loving too many men and one of them persuaded her to engage in a few hold-ups with him. Yes, they are all very much in love with each other. Perhaps I've refrained from loving because it always seems to lead to some crime or other, and you can't even be sure of yourself, you know."

"That's a clever way of not answering me," she replied. "You know perfectly well that most men and women are much more peaceful in their affairs with each other. If they weren't, life on this earth would last about three weeks or so. You simply come up against the most exceptional and sordid cases, where the people forgot to be cowardly and hidden about their feelings. Part of the world is just a little more insane than the rest of it, but it's a small part on the whole. I want you to stop your wriggling and answer me. Have you ever been in love?"

"You remind me of a line I heard in a rotten play last night," he said. " 'What right have you to ask me this,' said the heroine, and she seemed to be very upset about it."

"You're not quite so agitated, so we'll brush that

aside," she answered. "Put your little rapier down and talk natural."

He was silent for a short time and a frown died and reappeared on his face.

"Women of your kind have a troublesome habit," he said. "They keep on carelessly digging, digging into a man's heart, without realizing that they may be stumbling across old wounds that the man doesn't want to reveal, and it means nothing to them except a light sentence or two. I have loved two women in my life. One of them allowed her parents to force her into a rich marriage and the other one—the other one died just after we were engaged. . . . You go on in spite of everything, that's life, and you have duties and responsibilities that you must pay attention to, even when you dread the thought of returning to them. But you never forget. . . . You see, all of this means nothing to you and everything to me, and you simply sit here and tell yourself that you ought to be very sympathetic to me, but you're not. We can never really sympathize with anything that we haven't seen or heard ourselves."

This was the first time that he had ever dropped his authoritative worldly wisdoms and betrayed simple, warm sentiments, and she ordered herself to feel a little ashamed at the nonchalant way in which she had forced him to return to sorrowful periods in his past life. In reality, she was not deeply stirred. All people had suffered some time in their lives, or were still suffering, and their outside grief could not

affect you unless it was expressed with some degree
of fancy and individuality, so that it failed to become
an emotion which any other man or woman might
have had in exactly the same way. Otherwise you
took it for granted as part of the general, blurred
darkness beneath the top brightness of life, and you
had no real tenderness toward it, although you told
yourself that such a feeling was imperative on
your part. This man had passed through painful
episodes, but his words did not indicate that the
pain had left any restless aftermaths in his mind
and heart, or that it had given him any intensity of
despair, or of stoicism. He had gone on, with a
dull acquiescence beneath which he nursed occasional
twinges of memory, just as thousands of other
people did, and his pain had become no more than
a buried will-o'-the-wisp beneath the practical labors
and pleasures of his life.

"I'm awfully sorry for having blundered in this
way," she said. "I didn't want to hurt you, Syd, but
somehow I had come to look upon you as a man
entirely without deep emotions. You hide them so
well that it's easy to be deceived about you. I really
do sympathize with you, and my response is much
more real than you think it is, and I'll try not to be
so careless again."

Ah, the easy, soothing words that one uttered to
people. You felt that it would have been wrong to
withhold an inexpensive caress which might heal
another person. Or was it something else—was it

the endless, trivial double dealing pounded into you by your elders from the time of your birth—the constant admonishing that you had to regard conversation with another person as a veiled procedure, unless marriage or blood relationship gave you the right to be intimate and uncovered in your speech? This thing was called good breeding and refinement, and it changed men and women to the most inane of mechanisms.

"We'll only make it worse by lingering over it," said Levine. "Besides, it wasn't your fault entirely. How can one person know what's concealed in another person's heart unless the other uses a megaphone most of the time? We can't always worry about whether we're going to hurt somebody else, for if we did we'd lose the spontaneity that makes conversation interesting. You have put me in a frank mood, though, and I don't know whether I should be grateful to you."

He sat for some time without speaking, and Jessica was also silent because he had robbed her of the desire to say anything except words which she did not feel. Then he dropped his hand upon one of her arms and spoke in a clearly even voice, as though he were explaining a case to some judge.

"I have wanted you for six months," he said. "I have refrained from making love to you because I am a proud man and I didn't care to run the risk of your refusing me. I know that I am not usually physically attractive to women and I wanted to be sure that you would respond to me. I am still uncertain about your feelings toward me, but I've made up my mind to be candid with you. I have no lies or romantic pretenses to give you. My love for you is entirely physical, and nothing except complete possession will satisfy it. If you give yourself to me in that way, you will bring me happiness and peace——emotions that I have not had for several years. If you refuse to give yourself tonight I will bow to you without the slightest resentment and we will not see each other again. From now on it would be impossible for me to control myself in your presence, and it will have to be everything or nothing."

This was the first time that any man had ever succeeded in astounding Jessica. She told herself, incredulously, that she must be passing through some kind of phantasmagoria. Levine's abrupt, prodigious frankness fell like a blow on all of her emotions. Here, at last, was a man honest enough to dispense with all of the honored clap-trap with which men verbally pursued women, and to stand before her, naked and unadorned. She tried to feel repulsed, and then indignant, but the reactions were manufactured ones and they did not survive. There was an impressive simplicity about his request, and somehow it did not seem to be rude or coarse, although it should have been. It was one sex speaking to the other, without a trace of complacency or intimidation. It was the antithesis of what she had wanted

from a man, for it was completely without subtlety
and mental regard, and yet it did not repel her.
Why? Was it because at bottom she had been longing for such a plain, brave sincerity, beneath all of
her parryings with the varied lies of men's words
and beneath her standardized worship of poetic and
"artistic" ideals? No, her longings for decoration
and variety were real enough, and if she had been
accustomed to speeches such as the one that Levine
had made, she would have felt wearied and unmoved.
But as it was, she had grown weary of the fevered,
never-believed, poorly glossed protestations of men,
and Levine's crude words had been refreshing to
her. Instead of fencing with her skepticism he had
disarmed himself before it, and she was impelled to
respect him. It would be so easy to refuse him, and
if she did she would feel little satisfaction afterwards. He had spoken as though he had expected
nothing from her but was merely asking because it
was necessary for their relations to take a final
turn. Somehow, she knew that he would leave her
quietly and without another overture if she rejected
him, and that she would not experience the disgust
or enmity with which pride strengthens itself. For
once in her life she had a chance to become boldly
and completely understanding in a situation that
was not repugnant to her spirit. Some of the
curiosity that she had felt long ago came back to
her. Then it had been muddled by a youthful

bravado, but now it might be clearer and more compelling. She would never know what life really was unless she abandoned herself to it at least once with an unembellished, undreaming, and purely physical ardor. In this way she could test herself—find out what she really wanted. Levine, in a sensual way, was neither attractive nor ugly to her—he was a convenient instrument by means of which she could establish her elusive longings.

Over ten minutes passed silently before she turned and looked at him. Words are, after all, the nervous expedients with which people search for something that refuses to stand still, and when the thing becomes definite and motionless, words are then deserted because they have changed to mere, superfluous tensions. (Levine and Jessica rose without speaking and, with their arms around each other, walked falteringly to one end of the room. He had expected everything except her immediate affection, and had merely spoken to make an honestly hopeless farewell.) Now he felt dazed, and confused, and a little remorseful. Would it be quite fair to take advantage of the helpless spell under which he had evidently placed her? Was it honorable to let her disregard the consequences of what was impending? He had spoken so often of honor, and virtue, and of the unclean scoundrels who defiled women for no other purpose than that of flitting lust, and now he was about to ridicule all of his past eloquence because of a few words which he had wrenched from his unwilling heart while sitting in this room—because of a farewell that had turned out to be an astonishing reward. The touch of her face against his, however, instantly expelled all of his scruples.

Life held one, simple avalanche which you could not avoid.

He kissed her with the stunned hunger of a man who could not believe that something unexpected had come to him, and in a low voice he kept on begging her to speak to him and convince him that they were really together. She felt passive and suspended.

Afterwards there was nothing left for them except to say good-night to each other in a constrained, empty, doubting manner. He now became awkward and ordinary to her, and she longed for him to leave. He felt downcast and shaken, and could scarcely resist the impulse to ask her to marry him, both as an atonement and because she was now doubly intriguing to him, but he knew that his words would have sounded like a hollow and forced anti-climax.

When Jessica had retired to her room and was resting upon the bed, a slow revulsion rose within her. As she looked back on the past two hours she saw that she had been misled and defrauded by her own impossible dreams. Even in the midst of Levine's caresses she had said to herself: "Why can't I lose myself in this thing?" Her curiosity was dead now, and she felt certain that sex would never be anything more to her than a reckless striving followed by the throes of conscious defeat. Was this caused by a defect in her nature or was it due to the fact that she had not yet met a man able to reach the last depths within her?

The question could not be answered, and it increased her disconsolate mood. In addition, she felt that she was becoming an indiscriminate sensualist and using one excuse after another to dodge her realization of this rôle. She was losing the integrity of herself and receiving nothing in return. Soon she would be the subject of the whispered descriptions and confidences that men traded with each other—the thought repelled her. She had a wise head and weak emotions, and the head would have to govern her from now on. Since none of the men whom she knew were able to leave her at ease, it would be best to avoid all of them. She would meet new men, and have only the most casual relations with them, and never attempt to attract any one again until she felt overwhelmingly sure that every particle of him held an alternate challenge and surcease for her mind as well as her heart. Even then she would keep on measuring him and holding him at bay.

A voice within her said: "Ah, Jessica, I know you —you'll do nothing of the kind. You want the moon

and you'll never, never get it, and you'll be constantly
jumping into the air and falling down again," but
she derided the voice and said that she would dis-
prove its pessimistic confidence. "I'm going to make
the moon come down to me," she said to herself,
"and if it doesn't, I'll make a better one of my own
and put it in my head and feel beautifully lit up."
She resolved to shun all men for at least a month
and do nothing but paint and read, or mingle with
the girls in her crowd, for purposes of idle relax-
ation. On the next morning she wrote a letter to
Levine in which she told him that it would be wiser
if they failed to meet again, since the night had meant
nothing to either of them save a mistaken wildness.
Their parting had been dumb and prosaic and regretful, and if they met again, these reactions would
probably be heightened. She had no dislike for him,
but it was evident that they were not strongly and
subtly attuned to each other, and it would be foolish to reiterate an incomplete, impulsive occurrence.
She would always remember the humble frankness
of the appeal that he had made, and always treasure
it, but she did not care to spoil it by seeing him again.
She hoped that he would not think that she was
brutally fickle but would realize that human beings
were often swept away by delusions that died out in
the thoughtful glare of morning. She also hoped
that he would not believe that it was her custom to
respond to any and every man's pleading, but would
know that she had been led astray by a rare and

powerful dream that failed to live beyond the stretch of one night.

When he received the letter he mistook it for the message of a woman who was chagrined and hurt because she had given herself to a man who would not permanently value her. He admired her pride, and the events of the past night still seemed inconclusive and unreal to him, and he had a feeling that she had somehow managed to stoop to him and still remain remote. This was a taunt to his spirit to bring her nearer to him, and he recalled also that the few other women in his life had never stirred him in this way. They had been jolly, and warmly usual, and handsome at their best, but he had always regarded them as obliging subordinates. Even the two who had mattered so much more than the rest had never quite aroused his respect—they had been agreeable, helpless, bubbling-over children to him, and outside of their sensual charm had planted within him a desire to be a kindly tyrant to them and protect their faiths and ignorances.

He wrote Jessica a proposal of marriage, and when she failed to answer, he telephoned her again and again, but she refused to speak to him. Wrangling and explaining about past incidents over the telephone was too ghastly a procedure, and she was also a bit afraid that he might melt her into seeing him again. When he found that his efforts were apparently hopeless, he sighed and consulted the feminine names in his notebook. A beautiful woman

had given herself to him and had mysteriously with-
drawn, and you hardly ever seemed able to retain
that thing which you wanted most of all.   It was
useless to throw yourself against the fixed disappointments of life.   Well, there were other women
in the world, equally as beautiful.   Besides, how did
he know whether she was not in the habit of reiterating such nights with man after man?   He didn't care
to marry a woman who could be snared by any one.
At any rate, emotions were precarious luxuries and it
was best to give yourself to them as little as possible.
He wrapped his dream in a sigh and forgot about it.

For three weeks Jessica kept to her resolve to
avoid the society of men, and gave instructions to the
maids to tell masculine callers that she was "out."
She painted in her studio every morning, read the
latest novels of the day or played the works of modern composers on the piano during the afternoon,
with the occasional variation of a horseback ride in
Central Park, and went to theaters and concerts at
night.   Maringold, who had noticed the absence of
men and late home-comings, questioned her one night
at the dinner table.

"What's happened, Jessie?" he asked.   "You
haven't quarreled with *all* of them, have you?"

"No, they just fade away of their own accord, but
they never realize it, so you always have to take the
first step."

"Aren't you somewhat haughty, young lady?" he
asked.   "You seem to expect a man to be a kind of

impossible composite of all the virtues. You'll never find a chap who's wealthy and handsome and interested in all of this art stuff of yours. They don't run that way. You'd better pick out a nice, decent fellow who'll be able to buy you clothes without going into bankruptcy."

"That's a darling reason for marrying a man but I'm afraid he'd never be as generous as you are," she answered lightly. "What's behind all of this sudden concern of yours, popsie?"

"I met Ted Purrel downtown yesterday," he said. "He was complaining to me about your not caring to see him. Said he hadn't quarreled with you and couldn't make it out. All at once you refused to answer his 'phone calls. Now, you know I never mix in your affairs, Jessie, but I think you're very foolish in this respect. Ted's really one of the finest men I know."

"He's one of the stupidest men I know," she replied. "When you sit beside a man it takes something more than his pocketbook to interest you. Ted's a funny proposition—he has a mind and a soul in him but he hardly ever dares to show it to any one. He talks like the titles on a movie picture and expects you to believe them! Whenever I get to the point where all I want is to be kidded along in the latest slang, I'll go out on the street and pick up the first man who passes. You can't go wrong that way."

Maringold wondered what in the devil his daughter wanted anyway—some one who would talk like a novel and act like the inmate of a hothouse? She didn't realize that men who struggled with practical affairs throughout the day were not disposed to sit around and spout flowery sentences at night. Then they wanted to feel jovial and relaxed, and not pestered by discussions on the fourth dimension or the expansion of art during the Renaissance Period. The trouble with his daughter probably was that she didn't know what she wanted and was flippantly toying with this man and that, to hide her lack of decision. Again, these "art" philanderings of hers were temporarily blinding her to the sturdier virtues in human beings. Well, no doubt all of this dross had to come out of her system, and if he opposed her she would only become more angrily attached to her silliness.

"I'd like to see the man who could live up to your ideas," he said. "I'm afraid the good Lord hasn't made him yet. I've no intention of trying to interfere with you, though. We've got to find out things for ourselves in this world."

"I'm finding them out very rapidly," she answered. "I think the first lesson is about over, father."

Not knowing what she meant, he smiled uneasily and patted her on the shoulder.

When the third week of her seclusion from men was nearing its end, her resolve began to waver. It was the beginning of May and spring was throwing sounds into the air with a sportive, practiced, feigned indifference to the mean and sober regularities of a city—children's shrieks, peddler's wails, street organ clankings, river-boat moans, tree-rustlings, and drawling laughters—and whenever Jessica went out on the street these sounds struck her and gave her a shivering that was half pleasant and half woebegone. The lighter side of the old drama was starting again and daring her to overpower it. What was life anyway but a few courtings of experience in which your ego resisted and accepted the egos of other people without any greater reason than a longing for motion and change? Even the people who were most tranquil and smug had a touch of this restlessness, only they hopped on a train and went to a summer resort, or strode around a golf course, or flirted with some one in a street car, instead of really breaking away from the recurrences in their lives. If she intended to stop her contacts with human beings and remain immune to their supplications, and deceits, and frolics, and strivings, it would be better to slay herself. She had become a dainty, sterile coward, afraid that life might mark her and abuse her a bit before she died. She had been waiting for a transfiguring experience, but such experiences did not come to you in a semi-cloistered existence. What did it matter whether a thousand men touched her if the greater part of her remained an intact and distracted bystander? She would never meet a man able to pierce, and stun, and renew her unless she allowed men to throw themselves at her now and then, and show her their lusts and minds—you couldn't find out what men were by standing at a distance from them, and in that case the one man whom you wanted most was liable to pass unnoticed. Whenever she was disappointed by any man she became an artificial, horrified nun and acted as though she had contaminated herself, and withdrew to a supercilious loneliness, instead of shrugging her shoulders and saying: "Oh, well, one more blunder shot to pieces!" What was the use of pretending that she was not sensual when all of her past episodes pointed in the opposite direction? She wanted some one who could possess her without making her feel dismal and swindled when it was all over, and she would have to continue her hunt for him. If he never materialized, she would at least be able to tell herself that she had exhausted every means of finding him, and if the fault was her own she could prove this to herself only through repeated defeats.

A voice within her said: "This is exactly what I said you would do, Jessica. Your whole life is going to be a farce, and you'll keep on letting one fool after another take your precious body when you know in advance that the outcome will be ennui and disgust. You'll become coarser and more susceptible with each experience and in the end you'll be little better than a hypocritical and covered-up street walker. You're too egotistical to lose yourself in any man, and you'll go on seesawing between men and loneliness until you're over forty. Then you'll probably make a belated marriage in a last effort to conquer your boredom!"

Jessica listened to this nagging, bitter, frustrated voice and felt a consternation that faded out to a weary bravery.

"Well, suppose you're right?" she answered. "Will I be any better off if I shut myself up for the rest of my life? It would lead to an even emptier conclusion, except that I'd feel stifled in the end, and not satiated. In the meantime I'm going to prove that you're wrong, old sneerer, and I'll keep on searching in spite of you. Life's a careless, accidental, cruel free-for-all and we don't alter it any by creeping into a hole and letting it pass over us."

She returned from the stroll that she had taken and found a message from Gloria, reminding her that the street fair of the Jason League was to commence within a few hours and that she had promised to make sketches of people at the fair. A sprightly malice bobbed up within her, and once more she wanted to tweak the nose of life and murmur conventional sentiments while intently watching the results of her impertinence. She put on a gypsy costume and pinned a red rose to her hair and drove over to the fair.

Raised platforms had been erected in the middle of a boulevard, and they were framed by gayly colored booths and artificial shrubbery, with stairways leading from one platform to another, and strings of Japanese lanterns that would be lit when

night came, and red, white and blue pennants fluttering on the tops of the booths, and flowers standing in high, plaster urns—a muddled, papier-mâché,
vacantly garish effect. Pretty girls stood in the
booths and sold objects that ranged from cigarette
holders to table-cloths, with an emphasis resting upon
art-and-crafts work. Some of the girls strolled
among the visitors and disposed of raffle chances,
flowers, and balloons, while two jazz bands made
music that strutted and stumbled with a tense,
hilarious, carnal deviltry. The crowd consisted
mainly of society people and people who believed
that the coy glamour of society would come nearer
to them if they attended this "exclusive" fair, but
there was a sprinkling of other characters.

The services of several actresses and chorus girls
had been enlisted, and they wore their scantiest
street gowns and tripped with a merrily self-conscious, condescending, appraising air, or affected a
lounging and stilted demeanor. The sponsors of
the fair had felt that actresses would be valuable in
loosening the pocketbooks of patrons who would feel
honored by the chance to rub elbows with these
wicked, famous, beautiful creatures, while the more
sophisticated males among the patrons would flock
to the fair to invite these ladies to parties and midnight revels. You were justified in using various
clever expedients to further a worthy cause, and you
couldn't get away from sex, even at a charity fair.

The men in the crowd were business men and

young idlers, and all except the most venerable ones were there to give their sex a polite but attentive tour of inspection. Nearly all of the society girls were marriage anglers or almost-virtuous "teasers," who would permit nothing that was conclusive, but there was always one in every hundred or so who was known to be obtainable if the overtures were adroit and well-timed. Among the younger men, a sprinkling of well-dressed adventurers sauntered about. They were of a kind that prowl along the fringe of society and search for prospects. They claimed to be students of art, or dancing, or acting, and their sole aim was to find some woman, or a succession of women, who would each support them under the impression that she was aiding their careers. They walked from one booth to another without purchasing anything, and centered their efforts on the married society women, to whom they spoke with a loquacious deference and many pseudo-cultured phrases on the better class of books and plays. A few city politicians were in the crowd—men with broad shoulders and dull beefy faces—who had come to scan the "classier" girls in the one section of society over which they had no authority, and to increase their popularity as good fellows and heavy spenders. A scattering of detectives completed the masculine contingent, and they were there to protect the society people against being robbed and molested by a lower and irreverent class of men and women.

Jessica gazed at the assemblage with a slight but

smiling approval. Whenever she mingled in large gatherings of people she had a tendency to become thoughtless and conventional, as though another self within her were greeting its counterparts in the human beings around her. She grew consciously satisfied with herself and intent upon being praised and graciously holding people at arm's length. An automaton rose within her and suggested the most proper and least offensive remarks and retorts. It was as though she had been drugged by the qualities parading in the scene, with nothing remaining in her save the suavest dissemblings of sex, and expressions of good-will or harmless impudence.

She was immediately greeted by Mrs. Howard Farrington, one of the hostesses at the fair—a tall, stout woman with a roundly composed, fair-skinned face, dressed in an intricate, dark blue gown.

"My dear, I'd almost given up hope of your coming," said Mrs. Farrington. "You're frightfully late. I'll take you to your booth, and you'll find everything there that you need, except inspiration, but I suppose you carry that around with you. Be sure and, well, flatter them just a little, perhaps. I'm sure that in many cases you'll get more than the regular price, if you do."

"It's a funny world," answered Jessica. "Who on earth would imagine that there was any connection between helping poor cripples and taking the kinks out of people's faces."

"If you're going to get philosophical please pick

out some other place except a fair," Mrs. Farrington said, amused. "Every one's just as vain as every one else, but no one likes to confess it."

Jessica entered her booth and began to make ten-minute charcoal and pencil sketches of men and women, bantering with her customers and assuring them that they had some unique facial characteristic which made it a pleasure to draw them. If they seemed to know that they were not good-looking, she told them that they had very strong and unusual features. None of them even dreamt of believing a word of what she said, but they were not averse to the sound of her comments. Toward the end of the afternoon Purrel walked in.

After they had greeted each other, he sat down with a sulky, questioning air.

"I suppose I'm not wanted," he said, "but you'll have to endure me until you finish the disagreeable task of putting my face down."

"Ted, don't act like a baby," she answered.

"Why have you been avoiding me?" he asked. "You're the most mysterious person I've ever known. You've given me every reason to think that you care for me and yet you've been snubbing me for the past month!"

"I simply haven't been seeing anybody," she replied. "Don't imagine that men are the only concern I have in life. Besides, any one is apt to bore me if I see too much of him, and your conversation isn't particularly startling, you know."

"Oh, come down from that high horse of yours," he answered. "You're a delightful girl but you're not as far above other people as you think you are. Life isn't just sitting around and talking about this painter and that composer. When you get that art bug out of your head and start to be human again you'll have a much better time of it."

"It's nice of you to advise me," she said. "Whenever I'm feeling wretched and unstrung you come around and tell me exactly what to do, and then I feel happy again."

She was in a blithely thoughtless mood and his words were far-away differences in sound to her.

"You're always objecting to kidding but you hardly ever do anything else," he retorted. "I'll give a prize to the man who can hold a serious conversation with you. If I didn't really care for you it wouldn't matter to me. Then I'd just give you all your wise-cracks back again and forget about you."

"Don't be so se-ri-ous," she answered. "If you keep it up I'll add an extra inch to your nose. I'm feeling horribly malicious today. There, it's done now. The pensive features of Mr. Purrel immortalized."

"They'll be embalmed soon if you don't treat me better," he said, as he rolled up the pencil sketch. "There's a dance out at the South Shore place tonight. Come on with me, Jes'."

"I can't go tonight," she said. "I'll be tied down here until twelve at least."

Purrel was in one of his heavy, reproaching moods and she wanted lighter companionship unless the man had something new to say—a virtue which Purrel did not display.

"Well, how about a party tomorrow night?" he asked. "If you turn me down this time it'll be the last. I mean it, Jess."

"I know that you don't mean it so I'll go with you tomorrow," she said, "but if you're not less threatening and dra-mat-ic, I won't stay with you one minute. When you're trying to be humorous you're much more interesting."

"All right, I'm the bright little target," he responded. "The jester's going to amuse the queen for a night. As usual, you'll listen and say nothing, or next to nothing, and expect me to say everything. I'd have a peach of a mind in your estimation if I sat around and spouted one epigram every half an hour. Anyway, I'll be up to your house at nine, and we'll take in the cabarets, and you can bring another couple along if you want to. I made a little clean-up on Westinghouse Preferred yesterday."

Another customer interrupted their conversation and Purrel departed. Jessica ate supper at a restaurant that had been rigged upon one of the platforms and then returned for another two hours of sketching, at the end of which a group of girls and youths, including Gloria and Ethel Daniels, swooped down upon her booth. The girls were clad in fluffy, brightly pale evening gowns whose tops were cut low enough to show the first inch of a definite hint concerning their bosoms, and the young men wore black Tuxedo suits. When women are living in a time that is neither romantic nor swashbuckling, they expose their bodies more, because the men whom they know are too tired and prosaic to exert their imaginations in the matter, and require at least the beginning of revealment to make them succumb to the woman's charms.

The members of the crowd that invaded Jessica's booth were all talking and laughing at the same time, but their voices were never high-pitched and never without a trace of conscious manipulation. Smooth, shiny, and self-possessed, their faces seemed to be slightly different and yet much the same, as if an almost identical quality had been barely disarranged on each countenance—an animal deceit which trifled only with those thoughts which could be most useful for its purposes. The merriment of these girls and youths swept Jessica into its rhythms. An imp could take all of her dark complaints and investigations! Life was made for animation and enjoyment.

Gloria introduced her, among others, to a tall, stalwart young man, who had the smallest of brown mustaches curled up at the ends, and balanced features, and keenly shifting eyes.

"You met Bob at my place a year ago but you've probably forgotten," said Gloria. "You always do. You ought to have a card-index system, like I have— it saves you so much trouble. Bob's a perfectly wonderful dancer, and I'm going to spend the rest of the evening fighting you for him."

"Can't I throw up a coin and settle the thrilling combat?" asked Robert Valenter, the object of Gloria's threat. "That's a much quicker and more sensible way, and besides, it will keep me from losing either one of you, since you won't be able to blame the decision on me."

"I've never been known to dance with one man more than twice in succession," Jessica answered, "so you can cheer up and stop being afraid, and Gloria won't have to pull my hair out. I may give you the first one, though, just because I'm skeptical about your amazing talents."

"You'll violate your rule after the first and I'll be up against it anyway," said Valenter, laughing.

The group sallied to the dancing platform and Jessica revolved and strutted with Valenter and other men until after midnight. Dancing was a chance to forget tomorrow and yesterday, and become proudly joyous flesh that owned life and cared only for the night in which this ownership could be demonstrated. When she danced, her emotions were gleefully savage and filled with a confident hostility toward all of the prohibitions and remonstrances of life, and she passed into a condition where sensual caprices were alone supreme, while the music became an exhortation which she herself had devised, so that the notes and her steps became merged, creative units. The man with whom she danced, when he was a perfect dancer, guessed every twirl and urge of her mood so effortlessly that both he and she became a single conspirator. She had never really approximated the feeling of being possessed by any man unless she was dancing with him, for then all of the gross and awkward features of physical possession disappeared, while a less fierce but more complete surrender diffused her being. Valenter said innocuous, jesting things to her, while they were resting between dances, but his words were scarcely audible to her, and she brushed them aside with short and stereotyped answers. Why did he insist upon giving her verbal nothings when his silent animations were so much more expressive? Her idea of heaven was a deaf mute who would fox-trot with her every night and then vanish during the daytime!

When Valenter had taken her home and they stood in the vestibule of her house, all of her interest in him had departed. He was once more a tall man in evening clothes, with a sluggish brain and emotions that were obvious, and not satiated as her own were. She felt jovially empty and peaceful, and had a craving for rest, although she was still far from being physically tired. He promptly kissed her, and she looked at him without moving or speaking, and with a smile on her face. This encouraged his desires and he started to hug her, while his hands commenced the eager preliminaries of conquest, but she pushed him away with a firmness which he could not mistake. 'You're all alike," she said, placidly. "You can't re-

strain yourselves for the space of one evening, unless a woman's immensely uppish to you, and you
can never tell whether she's really responsive or not.
Don't you see that we've had each other so completely while we were dancing that anything else just
now would be absurd?"

He thought that she had been irritated by the
confident swiftness of his advances and that he would
have to persuade her that she really "meant everything" to him. Women liked to hear protestations
of permanent adoration, without believing them, to
make the submission to a man less common and hu-
miliating.

"You're misunderstanding me," he said. "I'm
really in love with you, in spite of the fact that we've
known each other for just a few hours. It must
sound ridiculous and untrue to you, and, oh, well, I
suppose you think I say this to every girl, but you've
honestly turned me topsy-turvy. You're the most
intelligent, and charming, and beautiful girl I've ever
met—I mean it—and if you'll only give me a chance
I'll prove it to you. I'm not just trying to have a
petting party with you. I've never been more serious
in my life."

"That's a pretty little speech—of its kind—" she
answered. "It's too bad I'm not a flapper about
eighteen—I'm sure I'd fall for it then. I don't want
you to think that I'm ritzy and sarcastic, but it takes
something more than a few sweet words and a few
hours of acquaintance to convince me that a man

really cares for me.   If you're so very much in love
with me, you can call me up at the end of the week,
and I might go out with you.   And now we'd better
say good-night to each other.   I'm very tired."

Valenter departed with a disgruntled feeling—
damn girls, you could never tell what they would
spring on you next—and this one was evidently full
of conceited whims caused by hosts of suitors.   Just
the same, she hadn't resisted his first embrace, and
the trouble was that he had lost his head and become
overhasty in touching her, and he could probably
land her if he was willing to pass through a period
of restrained pursuit.   Well, she was pretty and an
excellent dancer, and it wouldn't hurt to make at
least one more engagement with her.

On the afternoon of the next day, Jessica drove
down to Salburg's studio.   She had not seen him for
almost a month, and it would be distracting to jest
with his resentment and let him practise his hopeful
wiles.   Again, there was a bare chance that she had
misjudged him—at times he expressed a poetic defiance of the world that might be more real than she
had believed—and he was, after all, more verbally
entertaining than any other man whom she knew.
She had dodged the street fair by telephoning a
young art student friend and inducing her to act as a
substitute at the booth.   Fairs were all right for a
day, but from the second day on they became cheaply
skittish and prearranged—the first gayety fled, and
only an amiable endurance test stayed.

Her mood of yesterday had gone, and she felt thoughtful and perturbed. What was she gaining from all of these effervescences and prattlings to this average person and that? Was life so plentifully strewn with days that one could afford to waste them upon the idlest of self-abdications? She hated the duality in her nature that made her a flighty pagan on one day and a repentant, dissatisfied dreamer on the next. But was it a duality? In what way had she changed since yesterday? Instead of painting or reading, she was hurrying to another man, and the only difference seemed to be that a single self was looking for variety in other people because it had none itself. She sighed and dismissed the implication by resolving to study art in Europe during the coming autumn and finally "make something" out of her painting. She regretted that she had made an engagement with Purrel for the evening, and determined to bring Salburg along. The two men had never met each other and it might be diverting to watch their stolid animosity toward each other as each one courteously strove to minimize the sentences of the other man. Being well-bred, they would probably content themselves with moderated sarcasms and veiled inspections, but—when men began to drink they became crudely pugnacious or maudlin. Would it be wise to bring Salburg and Purrel together? Well, it would be agreeable to see some of Purrel's witless conceit driven out of him, and she would try to keep the party from drinking too much. The artist and the business man, each one ignorant of the other's language but pretending to be disdainfully conversant with it—it was too good to be missed.

When Salburg opened the door of his studio and saw Jessica, he gave a surprised hello to her sprightly words and then remained silent as she removed her hat and sat down. She had come to play verbal tiddle-de-winks with him again, after ignoring his telephone calls and a letter, and his best move would be one of careless rudeness. If it angered her, then she could depart—he had no more time to waste on this endlessly fencing girl unless she decided to change her attitude. He continued his work on the background of a portrait, which she had interrupted, and kept his back turned to her. She laughed to herself—this indifference was too silent to be real.

"If I'm bothering your work I'll come back some other time," she said.

"Yes, I wish you would," he answered, without turning to look at her. She felt angry and rose from the chair, and she was about to put on her hat when she decided that his own anger was more justified. She walked over to him.

"I've been shunning everybody for the past month and trying to get somewhere in my painting," she said. "I'm sorry for having neglected you, and you mustn't stay angry at me."

"Since you found it so easy to remain away from me for almost a month, you might as well make it permanent," he answered. "You never really think of any one except yourself, and I'm tired of performing for you whenever you have the whim to notice me."

"I ought to say good-by and walk out," she replied. "You're acting like a peevish child. Don't you ever get spells when you want to do nothing but work and be alone? Can't you ever live without seeing people all the time? Even the one person we like most of all can be forgotten for a time in the never-satisfied ache to express ourselves in some way besides talking and talking."

"You are trying to excuse yourself by dragging in another question," he said. "If you are going to regulate your life according to your own desires, without considering those of any one else, then you must not expect a man to run toward you whenever you wave your hand. I am not fond of being with most human beings, that's true, but there are two or three exceptions. I had included you among them, Jessica, but since your own feelings toward me are quite different, you had better not waste your time on me. You can find enough light, occasional conversations without my assistance."

For the first time she felt that she had actually hurt him and that she could not bob in and out of his life with a nonchalant irregularity, and expect him to be pleasant about it. If he cared for her to any deep extent, she must be tormenting him, and if he did not, his pride would naturally be even more averse to tolerating her seeming indifference. She was unfair to men and wanted them to accept her moods and absences with a cheerful silencing of their own impulses and needs, and it would be better to see none of these men more than once or twice, unless one of them mattered overwhelmingly to her or returned her own casual feelings. She decided that before she left Salburg this time she would find out whether she valued him more than any other man, and would remain away from him if she did not.

"I know I'm a selfish person," she said, "but it hasn't been that alone. I like you more than any other man I know, but it hasn't passed beyond that because I've been uncertain about you. Perhaps I don't love you because you haven't made me believe in the depth of your feelings toward me. Sometimes you seem to be just saying one thing after another because it's part of an old game that you've memorized, and I've never been sure whether I've been seeing and hearing Kurt Salburg himself or Kurt Salburg's technique toward another woman whom he'd like to have. Then again, I've been constantly wavering between the self that wants to play around with men and the one that longs to create and express itself. I'm an absolute mess in some ways, Kurt."

In spite of himself, Salburg felt guilty, and flattered, and speculative. So, she had been on the verge of loving him and had hesitated only because she had doubted his sincerity—a situation that merely asked his mastery to voice a native eloquence. Was her desire to create an honest and troubled one, and not a sighing pose, of the kind released by thousands of feminine dilettantes? Yes, she had a definite talent as a painter, and he could probably make it rise under his guidance, but he wanted a pretty, subdued housewife, or a passing physical affair, and not an artistic rival who would be continually pestering his own self-importance. Still, art was an impersonal, rarely exhibited struggle for beauty, and he had no right to discountenance it in any person. Perhaps it would be best to marry her, and help her in her work, and feel tremendously unselfish for a change, and again, after their marriage she might become gradually content to immerse herself in him. She was wealthy, symmetrical, fairly intelligent—what more did he want? Of course, he would lose his freedom among women for the time being, but he could eventually attain it again in the usual secret fashion. Well, there was no way of knowing how much you desired a woman until you had possessed her, for otherwise she might turn out to be a lifeless, awkward captive, or an apparent, over-humble mistress, without those twinkling caprices, and disheveled retreats, and erratic tendernesses, which could tease the regularity of your relations with her. He would use all of his energies to make Jessica yield to him on this afternoon, and afterwards there would be time enough to worry about the marriage question.

"I have no desire to be harsh to you but you have treated me as though you were hiring and discharging some footman or valet," he said. "On one week I see you three times, and then you are invisible for three months. Either I mean something to you or nothing—it cannot go on like this. You are always doubting my sincerity but you do not seem to realize that I have every reason for doubting your own. How do I know that I am not simply someone engaged now and then to etertain your vanity?"

"I've been treating you wretchedly, I know," she answered, "but it's been because I'm such an undecided, tormented creature. I never seem to know what I want and I'm just as cruel to myself as I am to other people. One side of me's constantly punishing the other side. Sit down and talk to me, Kurt, and forget that I'm probably not worth talking to."

"You imagine that your art and your sex must always fight with each other," he said, as they seated themselves upon the couch. "It is not true. Sometimes I think that art is only the distinguished way in which sex revenges its defeats and glorifies its victories. The great, indirect escape from personal life. Even the mystics and the intellectuals—what do they do? They take their sex and tear it up, and juggle with the pieces, and make a brilliant, difficult feat out of it, but the slightest turn in their daily lives can always put the pieces together again!"

"Page Mister Freud," she answered lightly. "He has a marvelous disciple buried in a studio in New

York and doesn't know it. Everything is sex—I've heard it so often that I'm tired of it. If art weren't an enemy of sex it simply wouldn't exist—people wouldn't care to write, and paint, and sculp, and let their sex torture itself a second time. There's not the slightest reward in such a torture, you know. It wouldn't happen over and over again, in every century, if it didn't spring from a fundamental impulse all its own."

"But art is an escape from one part of this cruelty," he persisted.

"An escape from what—from a visible cruelty to a less tangible one?" she asked. "I don't agree. When you're an artist you feel something in you that's stronger than sex itself, and if you didn't feel it you'd take the rebuffs and happiness of your life as they came, and esca-a-pe from one to another without worrying about paper and paint. That's what most people do, and the few who don't, they yield to a greater pain that stands outside of their personal life and derides it."

"Yes, they think that they are doing this," he replied. "It's a charming, fiery delusion, Jessica, and it's always necessary. Some people can deceive themselves in simple ways but other people, with more complex natures, they must find a less obvious method—art."

They continued the argument for some time and then suddenly became silent. Jessica was tired of words and wanted to forget all of their problems and ill-rewarded urges, and a hopeless peace rose within her as she propped a cushion on the wall behind the couch and leaned her back against it. It was better to live, and work, and play, without bothering about your reasons and tearing everything to shreds. Otherwise you simply retarded your bit of life without any decent compensation. Oh, yes, it was born within her to worry about herself, and she would probably never be free from it, but she could at least desert it for the rest of this day. Salburg, who had been carried away from himself during the argument, returned to his dominant hunger. They had been acting like windy fools when they should have been in each other's arms. You only talked to a woman when it was impossible to obtain anything more satisfactory, or when you had possessed her and were using words to celebrate the past occurrence. Ah, an ideal mistress would be one who would chatter to you on the street and in public places, and remain silent the moment you were alone with each other. Men and women spoiled their love and hastened its death by babbling until it became no longer mysteriously all-important but shrank to a feverish pause in the fruitless conversation

He dropped his hand on Jessica's shoulder and held it there for a time, without speaking.

"Well, I have no more protestations to give you," he said. "If you still fail to believe in my love for you, then no last words of mine could make you change. You have instinctively decided the matter in one way or another, and you would pay no attention to what I said."

Jessica smiled inwardly—sincerity and insincerity —what funny words they were. If you desired a man, his "sincerity" didn't matter to you, and if you didn't desire him, it was equally unimportant. Did she love Kurt Salburg? Another funny word—love. When you felt that you were better than a man, you bent down to him *if* he seemed to be wistful, and gracefully boyish, and not physically repulsive, and with a pleading nakedness in his words that somehow rang new to your ears. When you knew that you were much inferior to a man, you gave yourself to him with a dazed or anguished desire to become his equal by having him stoop to you. That was the kind of love that she had never felt and was always searching for. Was it a tempting myth, and did all women strive to feel it without quite reaching it, always waking up to find that they had missed oblivion and abandonment by the scantest of inches? She was still peacefully self-conscious as she rested upon the couch, and she felt a critical tenderness toward Salburg, as though she had found all of his words a little wanting but desired to comfort his distress and return some measure of his longing. She told herself that she could not be quite certain of her feelings toward him until she gave herself to him. Her present mood might be a prelude that would be entirely slain by the touch of him. Yet, was it always wise to give yourself in the hope that your first emotions would prove to be inconclusive and that you would be stunned and consumed by a burning self-forgetfulness? Weren't you risking much for a dubious return, and insulting the subtle exclusiveness of your body? Certainly, her previous experiences suggested that she was facing the prospect of another failure. She hesitated, and her heart slowly turned to a tumult of assents and forbiddings.

To Salburg, her long silence meant that she had capitulated but could not induce herself to say the revealing words, and that she wanted him to take the first step. He began to kiss her lips and cheeks, with an expectant and yet fearful steadiness, and she did not resist him but kept her hands tightly folded over her breast. His sleepy face became more concentrated and wakeful and his gray eyes were dilated and lost their heavy-lidded concealments. In the midst of his unbearable desires he paused to marvel at the strange commotion which had taken possession of him. No, he had never before felt quite this way about a woman. Even though his success seemed certain, he was still restrained and afraid that some false or over-quick movement on his part might defeat him. When other women had given him the first signs of submission he had always confidently advanced, with a little disdain at the final ease of his conquest, but now, in the same situation, he was still unimpressed by the evidence of his sight and touch, and felt that she might spring up from the couch at any moment and walk from the room. Yes, he must really be in love with her and not merely desirous of her physical favors—an inevitable retribution! All of the women whom he had taken so carelessly were probably condensed in Jessica's form and waiting to mock and deny him.

He was close to weeping as he sought to remove her hands from her breast without using his full strength, lest he should displease her.

"If you should refuse me now I would never live again," he said, in a low voice. "Never, never. I have lied to women before, and now, perhaps, I shall suffer for it. I am helpless and frightened, Jessica."

His words had a defenceless quiver that could not be disbelieved. They gave her an elderly compassion that assailed the doubting thoughts to which she had been clinging. A disrobed and frantic boy was speaking his fear that she might whip his naked breast. Why should she refuse something that meant incredible end of pain and denial to him and a grasping at the impossible to her? This endless withholding—what did any one gain from it? Her hands fell limply from her breast and her body relaxed, and for the first time his arms went around her in a tightening loop and he knew that he had somehow escaped from the expected revenge of life.

One hour later, as they sat in the twilight of the studio, Jessica's face held an expression of exquisitely blended relief and disappointment, and her black eyes seemed to be looking at wretched hobgoblins impaled upon the walls of the room—symbols of her own jilted emotions. Once more she had experienced the sensation of being divided into actor and spectator, while the acting part made every wild effort to persuade the spectator to relinquish his identity but only attracted his separate admiration; once more she had failed to become one with the spirit and longing of a man, and had retained all of her consciously maternal, unfulfilled feelings toward him. Would she never learn that she had made a dream which no man could satisfy because it was born from a deep lack within herself? Yes, she would tell herself for the remainder of her days that she was merely waiting for the human counterpart of the dream to appear, because she was unwilling to part with the last fragments of hope.

The one difference rested in her attitude toward Salburg as she sat beside him now. Unlike the aftermaths within her nights with Purrel and Levine, she did not feel resentful at his presence, nor did she long for his instant removal. The other two men had become futile and obnoxious afterwards, as though they were reminding her of an indelible mistake and were grossly unworthy of what she had given them. Her emotions toward Salburg, however, resembled those which she felt an hour before while listening to his last, imploring words. He was still an urgent, mildly appealing boy who had lost his acquired sophistications and retained nothing but a simple, nude longing. The only difference was that now, since she had gratified his longings, he was humbly resting in the thankful daze which she could not feel. Did this mean that she was almost in love with him, or was it because she had become inured to defeat and could no longer detest the man who had given it to her?

She turned to look at Salburg, and in the dim light of the room his face seemed to be composed and beaming, and his tongue moistened his lips now and then, as though he were relishing his memory of the past episode. Was he gloating over the addition to his list of captures? The thought irritated her, and Salburg the man began to interfere with the youthful spontaneity which he had shown her, but with a great effort she dismissed the insinuation. Then she tried to relax and forget everything except the coursing of blood in her body.

As Salburg looked at her he felt complacent and commanding, but her value had not been diminished to him. She was still as delicately desirable as she had ever been, and his depleted emotions were praying for the return of strength as they mused upon what their next contact with her would bring them. He could not remember any woman in his past who had not become fathomed, dismantled, and just a little less alluring to him at best, after her first, complete yielding, but Jessica was different. She still seemed to be promisingly intact, and he felt that he had merely taken the surface of her and that she had withheld the greater part of her spirit and body while skilfully appearing to offer it. He did not understand her but he could not quite admit this to himself since it would have belittled his mind. Evidently, she was a woman to whom warmth and prostration came slowly, fought at every step by her pride and suspicion, and requiring a persistent appeal from her lover. Yes, she was in love with him, but she was also flustered, and self-accusing, and not quite willing to confess this love to herself. He must also be in love with her, since he had possessed women fully as handsome and shapely as Jessica but they had never left him with all of his desires still nervous and unrewarded. Ah, love was an inexplicable trick. It caught you in the midst of your careful sport with this woman and that, and made you juvenile, and credulous, and impatient, and you began to evolve reasons for its existence, to hide the fact that there was no real reason. Jessica was an ordinary girl, burdened with a little artistic talent, coddled and a little snobbish because she had too much money, and not even as pretty as two or three other girls whom he knew, yet she had shaken and baffled him, and he craved even the flitting touch of her fingertips. He would ask her to marry him, but not yet—he must be sure of his feelings first, and if he were too precipitate he might give her the impression that he had been wooing her with a secret glance at the material benefits.

They started to talk to each other—the inconsequential, perturbed remarks which a man and a woman make when they are seeking to readjust themselves and quell the after-effects of intimate physical relations. The past intensity has subsided and they must strive to feel that nothing has happened, unless they are unusually dull-witted or calloused, or unusually in love, for otherwise they would object to the betrayed uselessness of each other's physical presence.

Jessica and Salburg dined at a "bohemian" restaurant in the neighborhood of the studio—a place where bright colors, rough, wooden tables, candles, and futuristic designs were held forth as a bait for the frail imaginations of slumming parties—and with the return of their appetites life settled down to a merry, undisturbed, word-parrying affair. Then they drove up to Jessica's home, where Purrel was waiting in the main reception room. After introducing the two men, Jessica went upstairs to change her clothes, and they were left alone with each other.

Purrel felt angry and nonplussed by the strain of concealing his feelings, and he had intended to follow Jessica out to the hallway and berate her, but she had disappeared too quickly. What did she mean by bringing along an artist "nut" and spoiling their evening? He had told her to invite a couple, if she wanted to, but not a third man who would compete for her favors. She was beginning to believe that she could treat him in every careless, disparaging way and still depend upon his pursuit, and he would have to bring her to her senses. She cared for him, of course, or else she would never have given him all of herself, but she wanted to put him through an extended course of begging gymnastics before she became serious with him, and he had no intention of tolerating it. He would warn her that a repetition of this evening would cause him to avoid seeing her until she promised to behave in a different manner. As for this other fool, she had probably not informed him of her previous engagement and he wasn't to blame, yet the man had an uppish, subtly offending demeanor.

Animosity between men is often not the result of any spoken words, or definite actions. Sometimes a first mutual glance will produce an ill-feeling that persists in spite of all the subsequent, friendly words and the lack of tangible reasons. Each man feels that the other is entirely unlike him, and that he is being confronted by an influence of lesser quality within himself, and that he will never be able to rest content until he succeeds in demolishing the other man in some shape, thus proving his own superiority. The feeling is only partly instinctive, for two men, with their facial outlines, expressions of eyes, clothes, and the carriage of their their bodies, can manage to convey a clear message which no words or actions could possibly dispel. When, on the other hand, their words and actions fit into the more silent revealment, the result is a huge and immediate hatred.

Salburg was dressed in a neatly pressed, black suit, but there was a slightly disordered appearance about his collar and tie, and his shoes were not thoroughly polished, and one of the buttons on his coat was somewhat loose. Purrel, clad in formal evening clothes, sneered to himself at the faults in Salburg's attire. These artists affected to despise the customary styles and decencies in clothes because it enabled them to look down on other men, but they were as vain as roosters in every other respect. It would be embarrassing to go to a "swell" cabaret with a man not dressed for the occasion, and people at the other tables would stare at them and make ridiculing comments. Damn Jessica and the trivial loons that she insisted upon picking up! This man probably uttered the strained epigrams that she was forever prating about and gave her the cheap, unmasculine flourishes that she seemed to prize so much. It wasn't that she really liked these things—at bottom she was a wholesome, regular girl—but she had an inordinate love for flatteries, and fine speeches, and the small jewelry of life, because it pleased her highness to imagine that she was the great, original object to other people's eyes and ears. Well, it would have to be slowly knocked out of her. In the meantime, the small matter of this yellow-haired fool had to be dealt with. If Salburg became "too gay" with Jessica during the evening, he, Purrel, might not be able to contain himself. He would find out whether this man's fists were as able as his words—most of these artists wilted down when it came to a physical encounter. Let Jessica see what her precious high-brow was made of. It might also be an excellent move to refuse to pay Salburg's part of the cabaret bills—these artists hardly ever had any money with them and relied upon other men to meet the expenses.

Salburg, on his part, regarded Purrel as a blustering, well-clad cipher and resolved "to show him up" verbally before the end of the evening. Jessica might be inclined to be lenient toward this man because he was a wealthy member of the social world which she had been taught to respect, in spite of the scoffing words which she leveled at it, but her attitude would never survive after an exposure of the man's most minute stupidities. These upper business men, whose sole gift was the ability to pile up money through minor forms of cunning, thought that they were better than artists who placed the dash and color and meaning of life upon canvas. The artist himself could easily descend to their game, but he usually refrained because it made him feel too nauseated and microscopical. How these men patronized you, and waved their money in front of your face in an effort to restore their endangered egotisms! Often, they had the effrontery to pretend to be a part of your world, with their dabblings at painting, spurious Rembrandts and Corots, grand-opera boxes, and art institutes, and they could sit beside you and tell you exactly what art was and was not.

At first, the two men conversed about safe subjects such as baseball, the rotten, crowded subway system, and the question of who would be the next President, but after ten minutes these topics petered out, and a wary silence came. Purrel found the silence to be more annoying than their previous conversation, for it suggested that he was afraid to voice his opinions to this man.

"I suppose you make a good income out of your painting," he said.

"Up and down," answered Salburg. "It depends on whether I can find some one rich enough to pay my price. I have quite a reputation among the younger painters and I never take less than three hundred for a canvas. The difficulty is that wealthy people scarcely ever know anything about art, while poor people are better acquainted with it but they can't afford to buy your things."

"Meaning the wealthy ones have no taste," said Purrel. "Well, I'm not so sure about that. They simply won't let every one palm off his painting on them and tell them it's a masterpiece."

It was a general remark and Salburg could take it as an insult or not, as he pleased. Salburg was unruffled at what he considered to be a tu' pence ha' penny thrust.

"Yes, unless the painting has the name of an old master signed at the bottom," he replied. "In that case they are eager to pay twenty thousand for the work of some art student in Paris or Milan."

"Well, it's possible to fool even the best of people

sometimes," said Purrel. "I'll admit that artists win the hand-painted, porcelain napkins when it comes to selling people something they have no earthly use for."

This was Purrel's first, direct sneer and Salburg grew lightly contemptuous and wondered why it had been delayed so long.

"You are a stockbroker, Mr. Purrel?" he asked.

"That's right."

"Well, I would like to give you some instructions on the value of certain stocks and bonds," Salburg went on.

"What do you know about the stock-broking game?" asked Purrel.

"Absolutely nothing, but in your opinion that should qualify me to talk about it," answered Salburg.

Purrel grew hot beneath this sarcasm but determined to laugh it off, since the reception room was not an appropriate place for words that might lead to a physical battle.

"Neat comeback," he said. "You started it with your dig about wealthy people so I had to return the compliment. I guess we'd both better stick to what we know."

"That's not a bad idea," answered Salburg, glad that the boresome tilt was over.

They conversed for another half hour about the radio craze and the miserable programs at different broadcasting stations, a subject which Purrel had selected as one least likely to incite an argument, and then Jessica came down, dressed in an evening gown of mauve and saffron velvet-chiffon and looking as though she impishly sensed the words which the men had exchanged with each other. Purrel greeted her with a strained boisterousness, in his effort to hide his anger and because the anger itself was beginning to die at the sight of her softly desirable face and the half-uncovered, upstanding curve of her bosom. Salburg was silent, except for those bland monosyllables which he had to utter to protect the silence, and he told himself that he was facing a stilted, senseless night. It was one of those tiny purgatories which you had to contend with in your chase of a moody, pampered woman, especially if you loved her, and since the chase had practically succeeded, he could be forgiving on this night. He would try to become as witty and distant as possible, and crush Purrel's remarks without seeming to be disagreeable or unfriendly, and treat Jessica as though he were genially sympathetic toward her position as a buffer between two contestants.

Jessica was intent upon pitting Salburg and Purrel against each other because she felt empty, and half regretful at her afternoon, and wanted to erase the memory of her recent submission with a willful, hard-to-please, untouched air, and take the attitude of a woman unexpectantly waiting to be entertained. She wanted also to see how Salburg would react to Purrel's heavy repartee and she hoped that Purrel

might transcend himself and exhibit some of the
latent mentality which she believed to be in him.
This hope was not due to any emotional leaning toward him but merely because she feared that the
night might resolve into a dialogue between herself
and Salburg, with Purrel clinging to a glowering and
nasty mien. Her emotions toward Salburg had become uncertain. They were playing with remnants
of tenderness and wondering at their transformation.

Purrel's car was standing outside and the three
entered it, with Purrel at the wheel and Salburg and
Jessica seated in the rear. Purrel extracted a silver
pocket flask and offered it to Salburg, who accepted
it readily. After the men had taken their swallows,
Jessica insisted upon joining them, and they laughed
at her deep grimace and slight coughing after she
had placed the flask to her lips.

"You will drink Scotch straight, eh," said Purrel.
"I'll bet you're burning up inside!"

"I'm such a cold proposition most of the time that
it won't hurt me much," answered Jessica, intent
upon gayly saying nothing in the most impudent
manner.

"I'll say you are," Purrel replied, as he drove up
the street.

During the ride to a parking square in the theatrical district, Jessica and Salburg spoke about current
painting exhibitions and obscure, emerging artists,
with a nervous attempt to be impersonal, but Salburg's face was tight with suppressed begging, while

Jessica looked worried and pitying as she reproached herself for being unable to respond. After parking the car they went to a cabaret known as "The Golden Slipper"—a large, bright, ornately arrogant place, with a miniature stage at one end, a platform to one side of the stage holding ten jazz musicians, and a central dancing floor around which the tables were ranged.

The place was decorated in gold, black, and vermilion, and the walls bore frescoes in which a naked maiden wearing a golden slipper was pursued by a long-cloaked prince and his henchmen, who followed her on white horses through a forest and finally carried her away—second-rate, academic execution with a touch of Russian, garish simplicity. Clusters of electric lights shaded by little, golden-slipper effects hung from the low ceilings and were reproduced on the tables. At a first gaze, the bare, suavely glowing arms, shoulders, backs, and throats of women, with their pale-brown, pinkish brown, cream, and whitish pink tints, superseded everything else—sex, revealing just enough of its visible self to deepen the enticement and rescue the threatened mystery of the covered part. Modesty as an innate trait does not exist in women, but some degree of it must always be simulated to prevent sex from becoming monotonous, dully frank, and self-bored, and the difference in this respect between a prude and a courtesan is that the former is less modest because her denied sex placates itself with a constant, conscious advertisement. The women in the cabaret, with their bare throats and upper bosoms, were more modest than they would have been if they had draped every inch of their bodies, for this quality is the reflective hovering of sex between the extremes of nakedness and full concealment.

The faces of the women were much less individual than their bodies, as though slightly varied wax heads had been placed upon a medley of uniquely living forms, with the heads borrowing an unreal animation from these forms through a secret mechanism in the throat of each woman. Only here and there a face broke forth from the rest and looked openly contemptuous, or wistfully inquiring, or naughtily tender, or fearlessly gay. For the most part the faces had a sleek, emptily pouting, affected, bargaining expression—women intent upon extracting favors from their men and delaying the return gift until the end of the evening, or upon avoiding this return. There were petty battles at many of the tables—one woman sparring with three men in the process of selecting one for the night's finale, and two women contending for one, complacent man, and one man fighting to keep his feminine partner from being carried off by several other men—all of it veiled by an amiability that needed only an extra push to become an undisguised quarrel.

Unlike the women, the bodies of the men, in a dark uniformity of evening clothes, were unvaried and characterless, and denoted nothing save brawn or weakness, while their faces were more at odds with each other and showed more definite and nude degrees of greed, lust, anger, and sportiveness. When a face emerged here and there among the men it was because its careless joviality stood out against the calculating smiles and tensions on the other faces. Most of the men, carefully and with all the subtlety at their command, were gambling for women or for the good-will and influence of other men, except in those cases where the man had become drunk and was pugnaciously or mawkishly expressing his real emotions. When you looked at the scene, as a whole, it seemed forever on the verge of becoming an orgy and forever held back by fear and speculation. Certain effeminate men and masculine women were scattered about the tables, and they acted more spontaneously because their emotions, delicate and easily dismayed, shrank from the heavier and more hostile deliberations around them.

The head waiter, a partly bald, hard and yet affable man of forty with a face that barely missed brutality, who knew every wrinkle on Purrel's countenance, escorted the party to a choice table next to the dancing floor and near the stage. Jessica felt giddy, and ruthless, and fickle, and she began to scoff at everything that the two men said while still preserving an undercurrent of: "Oh, you know I don't mean it!" A noted Broadway actress, Violet Mayes, was seated at an adjoining table—a slender, young woman, with blond, artificially waved, bobbed hair, and a pretty face that had something of a wise, tired kitten upon it. Jessica and the other two heard Violet say to a fat man beside her: "First he takes one drink, and then he takes five, and he acts foolish, and the head waiter laughs at him."

"I'll bet that's the same one that laughs at Ted," said Jessica. "Do you know what Mister Purrel does when he gets drunk? He starts to recite lines from "Hamlet"—it's the only poetry he knows—and uses a straw for a sword, and tells the poor waiter he's an avenging ghost!"

"I'm going to do some avenging tonight," answered Purrel, "but it won't be ghost-like."

"Wait till the end of the night and then I'll let you murder me," said Jessica. "I refuse to die until I've had at least twelve fox-trots."

"I'm not longing for revenge or death," said Salburg, "so I feel a little out of place. Perhaps Mr. Purrel will tell us whom he intends to slay."

"Oh, it isn't you," answered Jessica, lightly, before Purrel could speak. "I'm the marked person in this case. Ted's jealous of me because I use only one variety of slang and not six, and paint terrible, grotesque pictures. He's the most indisputably normal man I've ever known."

"I certainly am and I feel like sticking to it," said Purrel. "You and Mr. Salburg can keep on making toys and hating money, and I'll go on raking it in!"

"It isn't necessary to love or hate money," Salburg replied. "If it's the only thing that you've been able to accumulate you're compelled to like it, but otherwise you can be indifferent to it most of the time and follow other mistresses."

"That sounds like a pose to me," said Purrel. "I always notice that the men who sneer most at money are never the ones who have much of it. Whenever I hear a rich man knocking it down, I'll pay some attention, but not until then."

"Yes, I am a poor man as the word goes," Salburg answered, "but I'm quite satisfied to be one, as miraculous as it may seem to you. I certainly wouldn't refuse wealth if it came to me, and I certainly ask a high price for my paintings, but the reason for my being alive has nothing to do with money or the lack of it. You make a certain amount of concessions to a practical world and then immerse yourself in more creative matters."

"Well, you're the doctor," said Purrel. "Maybe you're not quite as happy as you say you are, but there's no way of proving it. I'll make a bet, though, that you'd never be willing to starve for your paintings if you never sold them. You'd certainly be a fool if you did. Going after money is just as much of an art as going after anything else, and you've got to have a natural ability at it or you'll be out in the cold."

He was finding it hard to voice his animosity in the face of Salburg's calm disagreements—if the man would only "get personal" there would be an excuse for rancor and fisticuffs. Salburg felt the poorly hidden threat in Purrel's words but told him self that the other man was only indulging in a customary bravado. Jessica by this time was in a mood of jaunty indifference to anything and everything.

"This profound dialogue about money doesn't thrill me in the least," she said. "Both of you have no choice in the matter—you've got to defend your differences and you're not doing it very adeptly. Besides, I came here to dance. I'll do the first two with you, Ted, because Kurt doesn't fox-trot half as well as he paints. Don't be angry, Kurt."

"Oh, I'll try to live in spite of the deficiency," answered Salburg.

The evening was wearying him but he had become lightly resigned. The two men alternated in dancing with Jessica, and after Purrel's pocket flask had been exhausted his whisper to the waiter brought him a pint bottle of whisky which was "ditched" underneath the table. Jessica drank sparingly because she wanted to keep her senses and watch the two men—there was always a chance that the liquor might make them crudely quarrelsome, in which case she would have to act as a whimsical peacemaker. As Purrel continued to drink he became more loudly aggressive and yet said nothing that Salburg could construe as a plain affront. Purrel was still waiting for Salburg to make a clearly offensive remark, and he wondered how he could provoke such an occurrence without using profanity or invectives. Salburg grew stoically amused with each succeeding drink and joined Jessica in disparaging descriptions of the stiffly, weirdly smiling cabaret girls who were kicking up their bare, firmly rubbery legs and swaying their softly beckoning breasts over the dance floor as they shrilled a song entitled: "If You Do What You Do-oo, Half As Well As You Say You Do-o-o, You and Me Are Going To Get On Fine." He spoke to Purrel as seldom as possible, and tried to be vacantly agreeable.

Quarrels between men usually receive their final shove from some trivial, sudden incident which destroys the last shred of endurance in one or both men. As he turned to speak to Jessica, Salburg's elbow happened to overturn a glass of alcoholic lemonade and the liquid fell upon Purrel's trousers. Purrel rose from the table.

"You damn, clumsy misfit," he cried. "What do you mean by spillin' this stuff on me?"

Salburg felt an excruciating rage and stood up, with his hands clenched, but second by second the rage receded to a sick, shrinking, nerveless feeling. He remembered the time, years ago, when he had been ostracized and driven out of his regiment in Austria for refusing to fight a duel with a fellow officer, and the remembrance came back like a blurred but clutching harpy. The thing that he had subconsciously feared throughout the night had finally happened. He would have to exchange blows with this common, bellowing fool, and physical pain, the one thing which he dreaded most, would make him wince, and retreat, and grow heavy with a helpless self-hatred. Yes, the foul sharpness of pain would make his very soul curl up with cowering aversion and disgust, as it had done so many times before, and he would shield his head and step backward, and half-heartedly strike back at the furious hands that were disgracing him. Perhaps this time the first blow would transform him and sting him and sting him into a blazing lunge against this man; perhaps . . . but no, he had been through this thing too often. He would become bereft of all feeling save the punished longing to escape at all cost. He resolved to try a blustering attitude, in the hope that it might make Purrel afraid to strike him.

"This is not the place for a fight," he said. "The thing was an accident and you're not helping it by shrieking about it. If you're determined to be an insulting fool, we'll both step outside and finish the matter."

Jessica, who had experienced the first paralysis which surprise brings, leapt to her feet and threw her arms around Purrel.

"Ted, come to your senses, please," she begged.

By this time Purrel had forgotten that language existed, and all words had risen to a growing roar within him, and nothing remained except a longing to annihilate Salburg. He unloosened Jessica's arms and flung her into the chair, after which he struck out at Salburg, hitting him twice in the face and driving a third blow which glanced off the arm

that Salburg had lifted to shield himself. Salburg
overturned his chair as he retreated, and raised his
other arm to protect his face. Jessica had a glimpse
of his face as he stepped backward, and his lips were
eerily twisted and moving up and down as though
they were trying to utter a silly, unendurable sentence, the eyes were glazed and dilated, and a strand
of blood ran from the mouth. For a moment she
felt a mingling of equally strong pity and aversion
toward this face and then the pity died and she
chanted to herself: "Salburg's a coward, Salburg's
a coward," as though she were still unpersuaded by
the sight in front of her. She had never associated
him with physical cringing—he had always seemed
to be a man who could greet any kind of assault with
a nimbly disdainful, forward motion. Now she felt
that she must be seeing his actual self for the first
time, and she became puzzled, and miserable, and
uncertain, and agitated. She had changed to a blank
concerning Purrel and she did not know whether she
hated or admired him for what he was doing. He
was an angry automaton engaged in demolishing
her previous image of Salburg and bringing forth
another one.

Several men from adjacent tables had rushed forward in an effort to separate the fighters, and they
formed a milling mass beneath which Purrel and
Salburg could no longer be seen. Suddenly, Jessica
saw herself mixed up in the aftermath of this episode, with policemen firing questions at her, and

newspaper men waylaying her for interviews and photographs, and other people regarding her with a sneering suspicion. She was seized by a disgusted desire to flee from the scene—these two men had not given her the slightest consideration and they did not deserve her loyalty, and she would not be of any assistance to them if she remained. She hastened from the tables and managed to reach the outside lobby of the cabaret without being stopped, since almost every one was looking at the still struggling cluster of men, some of whom had drunkenly started fights of their own, while a police whistle was squealing outside. She hurriedly secured her wraps and departed from the cabaret, hailing a taxi-cab at the entrance.

When she had disrobed and was resting upon her bed, a cold dislike for both Salburg and Purrel mounted within her. The entire masculine sex separated to a physical bully and a physical coward, and each was as repugnant to her as the other. Some men imagined that they could obtain what they wanted by using their fists to defend the feebleness of their minds or the snubbed eagerness of their hearts, while other men, with stronger minds, employed more subtle and dodging methods because their bodies were unwilling to join in the conflict. The ideal combination was a man with a poetic, delicate, and original spirit, who could nevertheless be unflinching when faced by physical attack and abuse —a man who would fight only when the other man forced it upon him, but would fail to retreat in such a situation. Where did one meet such men—only on the pages of hectic, concocted novels? Were all of them weakly gentle or stupidly cruel? Perhaps the very qualities that made a man's heart and mind unique and fertile drew their payment from his body and caused this body to become drained and fearful. Perhaps it was inevitable that an exceptionally sensitive and finely wrought man should look upon physical combat as a degrading, resistless nightmare. She remembered her glimpse of Salburg's tightly sundered, retreating face and she pushed it aside as though she were pityingly but determinedly expelling a suffering child from the remainder of her emotional life. As for Purrel, he had tried to relegate her to the position of a woman who could be delighted and impressed and intimidated by the ruffian within him, and the liquor had encouraged him to desert his blatant thoughts and fall back upon his yelping self. The fact that he had been half drunk did not excuse him, for she had been to cabarets with other men in the same condition and they had controlled themselves under far greater provocation. She decided never to see either of these two men again, and to immediately apply for a renewal of her passport to England, a country where she would be removed from their pleadings and intrusions. Besides, she needed a new scene and new men to restore her tranquillity. Weary and relieved at this decision, her thoughts trailed off into sleep.

PART TWO

PART TWO

THE ocean was in a ponderously mild mood and lengthy, grayish green swells barely rose and fell, as though the water had fallen asleep and was unaware of its motion. Spots and streaks of sunlight in myriad arrays shifted and vanished upon the smooth water so swiftly that they seemed to be a madman's lavish exhibition of flimsily abortive fancies, and in the distance the light became an empty, vastly circling glare. The intensely pale blue sky arched itself above the water, and it was superbly detached and had no knowledge of anything except the slow-moving, fiery blotch of the sun.

Jessica reclined in a steamer-chair on the second, covered deck of the ship, near the railing, and she had a drowsily hurt look on her face—remembrance reduced to an irregular dream by the weary nods and indifferences of her mind, and the sleepy stirrings of her heart. The past complaints, wraths, joys, and aversions of men and women whom she knew bobbed up in her mind and seemed to be without meaning or purpose—people reaching for and avoiding shadows, shadows because it would have been unbearable to stand still, and making these shadows solid and real with an alternate fury and softness of talk and movement. This idea was not distinct within her, but it functioned as a part of her hopeless removal

from the previous clearness of life. As she rested in
the chair, life took on a jumbled, discredited, and
stupidly insistent aspect.

She was dressed in dark purple organdy with
white rosettes at the waist, stockings and shoes of
the same purple hue, a long, thin cape of white
velvet, and a pale straw turban trimmed with black
satin. Outwardly, she seemed to be an average,
fairly tall, half plump and half slender young woman,
who was either wealthy or knew how to ape the
suavely synchronized attire of wealth, and her face
at a first glance was not strongly individual but
merely verged upon a possibly smug prettiness, with
the cheeks a little too fully curved. It had a slumber-
ing, lightly disturbed look that might have been provoked by anything from a longing for the next meal
to the machinations of an absent lover. The visual
guise of human beings is never a reliable index to
their spirit and character, and even when the person
is dressed in a shabbily or richly unusual style, it
may be an unconscious or secondary eccentricity, in
no way related to his waking words and deeds. His
face may also be enormously misleading, as though
he contained qualities which life had refused to make
him aware of, and a thoughtless shop girl can often
look like the most meditative of patricians. The
fault, of course, is with the eye of the onlooker, and
it merely means that even the wisest of human beings
have not yet perfected a sufficiently subtle method of
deciphering the lines and garbs on other beings, but

rely too much upon the first, apparent indications. There are always little disputes in the appearance of men and women, if your mind is shifting and patient enough to catch them.

If you had looked long at Jessica, the smugness of her face would have grown more abstract, and you would have detected indentations of trouble at the corners of her mouth, and without knowing what it was you would have observed a haunting discontent within her black eyes. Bit by bit, your impression of a well-dressed, indolent pleasure-seeker would have died, and you would have been confronted by secret thoughts and distinctions beneath the deceptively composed, conventional exterior.

She had taken a second-class passage because, on a previous trip to England during a summer in her college days, she had found that the first-class section was apt to be filled with stereotyped travelers— lauded actors and actresses, who were perpetually smiling or sulky, according to their idea of which would be the best bid for attention; stolidly blank, wealthy business men and minor ones who wished to appear wealthy; members of the nobility, who walked around with an air of reserved investigation; diplomats and small officials, with worn, bland faces, who stayed in the buffet room and drank as though the next moment would be their last; society women and girls, who changed their gowns five times a day, played games on the upper deck, and gossiped in soft, modulated voices; a few professional men who had taken the trip to be away from thought and care and were always laughing with an uncanny strength of lungs; young men with the smoothest and emptiest of faces, whose occupation and status were negligible mysteries; polite, beaming housewives taking their first trip abroad and desiring to travel "in style"; and a few adventurers of both sexes, who mingled graciously with everybody and suggested bridge games or strove to ascertain your financial position.

Jessica had hoped that the second-class section would be less prearranged, with a certain number of more submerged and individual people contained within the preponderance of middle-class house-holders. A ship's trip was a sentence to a prison, and unless a few of the prisoners were unlike the liberated people whom you had left behind, you had the sense of dully plodding through an ever-lengthening stretch of time, with all of life dwindling to food, sleep, and the insufficient solace of your thoughts. She had discovered that the second-class section, on her ship at least, was just as stupid as the first but in a warmer and more impulsive way, and while there were no exceptional people, as far as she could see, those whom she met were more plastic and unaffected than the ones in the forepart of the ship. Disregarding the rule that sections must not mingle with each other—an ocean liner is a commercial obeisance to snobbishness and caste—she had sauntered once into the first-class region but had returned with relief to her own domain.

During her first three days on the ship, a young traveling salesman had told her how he had saved up his money to visit his parents in a German village where his dollars would be fortunes; a bubbling matron had drawn her into a discussion about the care of children; an old man had eulogized his dead son who had been in the war and whose grave he was visiting; a naïve college student had confided that he was going to see Europe "on his nerve," with little money, and intended to work his way back on a cattle boat in time for the fall opening of his school; and a vivacious girl, the winner of a "beauty" prize contest, had confessed that she was using the cash prize to travel to England in the hope of marrying some nobleman (her refined mother thought that most American men were so ill-mannered and common).

It was all funny, and pathetic, and homely, and filled with the now flitting, now fumbling dreams of most men and women. When she listened to these people, life was real enough to her, but when she sat alone on the deck, or retired to her cabin, she felt that these people interested her only because she had not become intimate with them. When you drew close to people, their ideals and hopes were somehow rubbed away, and each person disclosed a sordidness, or ignorance, or cowardice, which caused you to turn away from him. No, she was growing pessimistic and stale. Regarding the millions of people in life, she had met only a minute fraction and was using it to judge the whole. Besides, this easy habit that she had of calling other people cowardly and brainless—was she herself so brave and intelligent? She had gone to college, and chattered and danced at functions and parties, and mastered the piano just well enough to stagger through the works of modern composers, and could hold at least six glasses of whisky or gin without losing control of her legs and her mind; and was just above the status of an amateur as a painter—small accomplishments! And, oh, yes, she had forgotten—nonsensical skirmishes with men, including Purrel and Salburg. She made a moue at the latter two and hoped that they were consoling themselves with less exacting women.

Before her departure, Purrel had frantically telephoned, and ambushed her outside of her doorstep, but she had informed him that she didn't care for men who became boorish and snarling whenever they ran across the peaceful challenge of another man, and he had finally desisted, in an outraged spirit. Well, if she was so damn fond of yellow, mincing men she could have them for all that he cared! Salburg had written her a letter—an abased letter, by turns violent and imploring, in which he asserted that he had not resisted Purrel because of his desire not to involve her in a public brawl, and in which he swore that he would kill himself if she failed to see him. She had written a placidly motherly reply, in which she had told him that he wasn't a coward, but was not quite masculine enough to appease her more feminine side, and that she did not love **him** because he and she were too much like each other in some ways and too little in others, and that he should not have become melodramatic in the hope of frightening her emotions into a meaningless response. After reading and rereading her letter, he saw that further importuning would be useless, and he cursed himself forlornly as he went back to his more complaisant women.

Sitting on the deck of the ship, Jessica remembered her last afternoon with him, and sighed. The touch of his body against her own, and the moist trailings and lingerings of his lips upon all of her face, and the possessive weight of his breast, and his inquisitively destructive hands—what had they meant to her? Where were the mad, upward flights, and shivering collisions of nerves, and outbursts of light, and indescribably barbed pain and pleasure, and emptied peace that she had read about and longed for? Oh, yes, to be sure, there had been an eagerness to be stunned by the demented, hungry child which the man had become, and spasms of nervous release, and an after-feeling of beaten inertia, but everything had been completely physical, and never quite free from consciousness, and ever asking for an obliteration that never came but made you redouble your efforts to grasp it. Men and women were forever raving about this thing, and calling it bee-oo-ti-ful, bee-oo-ti-ful, and gasping over the starry heights and perilous ecstasies which it contained, but perhaps they had no choice.   Perhaps they were forced to idealize and magnify in words something that never satisfied them, because they wanted to forget their endless bondage to flesh and believe that they had risen above mere legs and breasts, just as the strict moralist tried to forget his own defeats by punishing and maligning these same physical embraces.   This was the reason that they had made a word—love—something to be cherished, and exalted, and obeyed in spite of the ever-recurring failures of their sexual emotions.   But women and men who were more stupid and coarse, and who disregarded this word, were better off.   They entered their rooms and were only intent upon giving something that could be seen and felt between the walls of the room, and had no dreams that could be killed or weakened by the morning light, but used every device that could bring them physical pleasure and then subsided dully until the next unglorified orgy.

Jessica said to herself that hereafter she would accept sex for what it was, without fleeing from it or ennobling it.   She went down to her cabin to dress for dinner, with a clearer head and a heart that had persuaded itself that it was indifferent to life.   On the fourth night of her trip, as she was resting on the berth in her cabin and reading a recent novel called "Jane Martin," she stopped in the midst of one of the last chapters and threw the book to the floor.   What a book of one-third truths, to which a realistic patter had been given to make them seem

moderately plausible! All of the girls were forever
kissing some man, and loving or hating him because
they would have wilted at the idea of being alone and
having nothing to fall back upon except their unmov-
ing minds—a crude delineation of the "flapper"
type—and being on the verge of having babies without the consent of marriage, and being happy or de-
spondent at the fact that they were about to give
birth to some one else who would (inferentially) also
run through the gamut of love, and kisses, and hazy
disappointments.   A dreamy, mercilessly verbose
youth named Roland wandered through the book
and uttered sociological investigations to pretty shop
girls in road house rooms, and hallways, and parks,
and was continually longing to be a pagan without
seeming to know just what a pagan was, or how you
became one.   The heroine of the novel, Jane, had
a much better conception of the word, and gave herself to several of the most tritely talkative men in
existence, and finally met Roland, with whom she
lived in an unmarried state.   Then she discovered
that she really wanted babies and a home, and Roland had the same odd longing, interspersed with
much reciting from Walt Whitman, presumably to
encourage the faltering participants, and they decided to be immediately married.

Ah, if life were only as simple and firm as that—
a few agitations, curiosities, and lusts concerning
this lover and that pursuer, and then a craving for
safety, and dull security, and the trusting ministra-

tions of children. Life was the profligate rivalry of ifs, and maybes, and whys, and yeses and noes, all of them promising you certainties and stopping you with doubts only to lead you to greater predicaments, and all of them fighting, fighting for your heart and mind and breath, and perhaps your soul, if you had one. Even the least receptive and discerning of human beings felt a little of this thousand-faced and -tongued commotion, no matter how much they tried to deny it with comfortable and orderly finales, and the novelist had caught nothing of it except the fact that men and women wanted each other's bodies and went about the task of attaining them, in bold, diffident, or talkatively roundabout ways. If that was all that life held, or knew, then it would have been wiser to stand naked on a street corner and bid for the most intelligent and comely passerby to come and take you!

Yet, the cry for babies rising from the novelist's pages made Jessica thoughtfully view a new question. Babies? Had she never thought of them before—outside of using practical methods to avoid them—because she lacked a maternal instinct? Round, diminutive faces, innocently, pertly puffed out, with something still and esoteric in their eyes, not knowing that life was unfair, and pointed, and luring, and wanted another batch of sacrifices—did she love them and long to hug them to her uncompleted breast? A stirring, a kind of "oh, go on Jessica, you must like them—everybody does," grew up within her, and then it was replaced by something between compassion and fear, and she felt that having babies was like making a second payment to life and pitifully daring life to defraud you once more. That was it. It wasn't that you wanted to leave behind a race of "singers, and workers, and warriors"—the wornout, poetic lie—or that you really hoped that your children would be more resplendent than you had been, or that you cared only for the selfish, brooding thrill of pressing a small head against you and letting its helplessness make you feel mighty—it was something outside of these things. It was your determination to let life know that it couldn't beat you so easily, and that you would conceive at least one human being, with something of your traits and beliefs, to carry on the hopeless fight. You didn't care to feel that you could be so thoroughly and instantly shoved aside. She had heard matrons say: "Oh, Harold is the liv-ing image of his father—I'm almost frightened at it sometimes—" and she had known that they would never rest until they gave birth to a child who resembled them. When people were articulate geniuses and were certain of it, they did not long so much for children because they knew that their work would remain behind and continue their resistance to life, but other people wanted to strengthen their sense of feebleness and escape from the extinction of physical death. Well, she would refrain from having children until she felt finally beaten and at the end of every other form of self-expression. In the meantime, she would cope single-handed with life and take its blows and ambuscades.

When she arrived in London, at the Waterloo Station, some of her relatives on her mother's side were waiting for her——Richard Swinson, and his wife, and Ruth, their daughter. Richard was an elderly Englishman who worked as a superintendent at one of the Lloyd banks and who had managed to come down because the day was one of the innumerable, minor holidays known to England. He was a short, beefy man, with the deep floridness that comes from an immoderate consumption of mutton-pies and ale, a low forehead, and thick, brown hair singed with gray. His nose would have been bulbous if it had not straightened a little just below his eyes, and his thin lips were doubled in upon each other, and his protruding, brown eyes looked at you fixedly and yet tried to protest that they were not desiring to intrude upon you. An expression on his face said: "You can't surprise me because I've learned all the tricks, I have," and he was a man who had made a fetish of calmness because it gave his undistinguished life the pose of a distinguished and liberally rewarded existence. Very deep within him, his emotions still hungered for fame and attention, but he fed them by strolling through Hyde Park, with a flower in his buttonhole and an intense swinging of his cane, or badly accompanying his wife on a violin, with all of the assurance of a great player, or by extolling his former prowess as a rugby-player. He was not an unkindly man but he could be unwittingly cruel in a case where he knew that the other person was superior to him but had not attained a rank or standing that could prove it.

His wife, Winifred Swinson, was a little woman who had been slender in her youth but now showed the flabby swelling-out that often comes to elderly people. She had been handsome once, and her high cheek bones, small, distended lips, abrupt nose, and large, blue eyes still definitely hinted at the past condition, in spite of wrinkles on her forehead and creases on each side of her mouth and the ashen skeins in her black hair. She looked as though she felt it a sad duty to be sprightly on all occasions and to counteract age with an overzealous assumption of youth, but this effort had become an increasing strain that frequently brought a flitting dullness to her eyes, and a droop to her lips, particularly when no one was looking at her. She was a practical, patient woman, who had never dreamed of more than wealth and an excellent house to preside over, and who had gradually contented herself with a modest approach to these objects. Her heart was at peace, except for small jealousies and envies that kept it from falling completely asleep, and her mind was something that counted the habitual occurrences of each day to see that none of them were missing or out of place. She felt that her husband was "a good sort," though rather inclined to preen himself foolishly at times, and whenever she read of divorce cases she patted herself at having picked out a steady, slow-minded man and not a fickle, brilliant one ("brilliant," to her, was attached to men who had been knighted by the King, or had gone to parliament, or had risen to high office in the church or army). She would have gasped if any one had asked her whether she loved him. Of course she did, and he was the dearest and most perfect man on earth, though naturally they couldn't act as wild about each other as they had when they had been young. Women of her kind, who have never experienced a deep and governing emotion for their men, feel the necessity for gushingly professing it more and more as they grow older, because they must have something that can take the place of the vanishing, sensual urge.

Ruth Swinson, her daughter, did not differ from the mother, although the contrast between them seemed to be strong. Ruth was the product of a more dashing and athletic generation, and frequently did things which disquieted her mother—playing tennis in a very short, wide skirt, or wearing an unusually low-necked blouse, or coming home from one of the dancing clubs at 3 A.M.—but at bottom her emotions were equally dwarfed and controlled, and she was determined to "have her bit of a lark" without going too far, and to keep her eyes open for a presentable, respectable man, not too old, and endowed with money and good manners. She was five inches taller than her parents, and they always seemed to be over-grown, masquerading children out with their governess for a stroll, as they walked down the street beside her.   She had a moderately plump body that was half symmetrical in a bluntly swerving way, and a pinkish cream, slightly freckled face that looked self-possessed and patronizing for no reason other than the fact that she was a young, fully curved woman and aware of it.

Women whose bodies and faces are the chief or only bounties that they have to give, and who have just wit enough to know it, must act as though they were condescending to exhibit themselves to eager eyes, for the thought of their being invisible to most men would become troublesome and discouraging. Ruth had her mother's blue eyes, and a nose that slanted straight downward and then bulged out just above the nostrils, as though both her mother and father had compromised about it, and full, firmly closed lips.   Like many middle-class, English girls at the start of their youth—she was twenty-one— she bore herself with an almost masculine erectness and ease, and walked with a long but not ungraceful stride.   She wore a gray linen dress, with a straw bonnet of the same color, and her father was clad in a baggy, lighter gray suit, and her mother was dressed in darker gray taffeta, and the combination made Jessica say to herself: "Well, I hope it's not too symbolic!"   Five years had passed since her first visit to England, and her remembrance of these people was not remarkably distinct, except that Ruth had been a dumbly silent girl then and the parents had been hospitable, and dull, and very secretly envious of their niece's money and varied apparel.

On the way to the Swinson home there was a flurry of commonplaces, exclamations, and questions about Jessica's father, and her aunt in America, and the kind of trip that she had had, and the length of time that she intended to stay in England. The Swinsons lived in the West End of London, in a place known as Tavistock Square, where two and three-story houses of red brick and dark stone enclosed a private park that was sheltered by high, brick walls, with only the inhabitants of the square possessing keys to its iron gates. Jessica reflected that in the center of the largest American cities you had to own your own grounds before you could have any privacy and seclusion in the company of grass and tall trees, and it occurred to her that one of the chief differences between England and America was that in the former country it was not quite so irksome to be poor, and not so much a spectacle of poverty swaggering about with shouts of democratic power while denied the least traces of leisure and space. She remembered that the slum districts in the East End of London, which she had walked through years before, had been as inhumanly crowded and dirty as those in New York City, but here, the few people who were lucky enough to graduate could move to the numerous private parks of Chelsea or the West End, while in New York City their goal was a cleaner but equally stuffy apartment building, unless they migrated to the suburbs.

She recalled another difference—the dwellers in the slums of London had been meek and more visibly chained, with the cheerfulness or sullenness of people who seemed to look upon themselves as a fixed, doomed class, as though centuries had rubbed their poverty in so effectively that it was heavily taken for granted. They had none of the noisy ambitions, and boasts of freedom and equality, and independent bearings, and studied apings of the finery worn by rich men and women, which she had noticed during her excursions to the tenement-house regions of New York City when she was taking sociology at college. Yes, this was the difference between England and America—in England, great masses of people nakedly accepted their fate, and in America they became dreaming, swaggering, childish liars and told themselves that they had escaped from this fate, or excitedly plotted to circumvent it.

But the Swinson family—the few, immediate words that she had had with them, aided by her reviving, past memories, told her that her relatives had the same complacencies, furtive snobberies, and material worships possessed by middle-class people in America. She recalled a passage from a book that she had once read: "The individual qualities of a nation can be found only in its highest and lowest stratas—in its aristocrats and geniuses, on one side, and in its proletariat and peasantry on the other. The middle classes of all countries are like each other, in spite of different mannerisms, because they represent a weighty average in the sum total of human thought and emotion—an average where all national and racial traits are fused together." She had memorized the passage at the time because she had proudly identified herself with "the higher stratas," and "middle-class" people had been just shopkeepers, and automobile salesmen, and hotel clerks, and modistes, who were deferential and voluble in your presence. Now, as she rested in the room assigned to her by the Swinsons, a first tinge of uneasiness came to her.

If her father had not been rich, what would she be—an adventuress, giving herself to men in return for luxuries and leisures, or a stenographer, hoping to be married to some man who could rescue her from the daily toil (without the aid of Whitman, as in the novel she had read on the ship!)? Being rich had been a condition so ingrained and matter-of-fact that she had scarcely ever thought about it, except to tell herself jocosely that being poor would have brought her more sexual risks and relishes, but now she asked herself whether she had any treasures outside of the unlimited funds that enabled her to indulge her whims and her doubtful bursts of self-expression. The six days of her trip across the ocean, where she had been forced to fall back upon thought as she sat on the ship's deck, had given birth to many questions within her. She trifled with a notion to discard her traveler's checks and try to earn her own living in England, and then she shook her head as she acknowledged that her spine was not strong enough for such an experiment.

If she had been more naïve, she might have looked upon the matter as a romping adventure, but she knew that she could never bear to receive orders and humiliations from other people and to have her hours at the mercy of one small task or another. No, her future was certain—a few more men, several canvases that would not be quite what she wanted them to be, and then marriage to some sturdy, wealthy nonentity. Oh, well, mooning about it wouldn't help matters much, and if by any miraculous chance it wasn't to be so, it would be caused by something outside of her mental anxieties and descend like a hurricane from a noon-day sunlight.

She dressed in an old rose crepe de chine gown and went down to join the Swinsons in their sacred four o'clock tea. The living room of the Swinson house was a mixture of Victorian bric-a-brac, antique, chestnut furniture, and some wicker chairs and bright curtains that were like a faint concession to modern ideas. She sat for a while, conversing about frocks and prices with her aunt and cousin.

"I saw a perfect wonder of a taffeta at Broughton's yesterday—trimmed with filet lace and Paris written all over it—and it broke my heart not to, well, not to be able to afford it," said Ruth.

For a moment, Jessica was about to say: "Let me get it for you," but she recollected that you often hurt people by seeming to rub in the fact that you had much more money than they did.

"I've been intending to give all of you some kind of present, just to celebrate our being together again," she said, uncertainly, "and I'd love to buy you that taffeta, Ruth. Please let me."

"Oh, no, really, I couldn't think of accepting it," said Ruth, "and you mustn't be hurt either, dear. I'd never feel quite right in something I hadn't bought myself. . It's a bit of foolishness, I know, but it's there."

"We do so like to be content with what we have," said Winifred. "It helped us to carry on when dear Richard's salary was very small, and we still cling to it. Then during the war we all had to retrench frightfully, of course, and we've grown quite accustomed to it by now. If you must give us something, Jessica, why any little article will serve. Richard's been wanting a new umbrella for ever so long, and he always forgets to buy one."

Jessica had been sure that her relatives were protesting to avoid having her think that they were humbly eager in the matter, but as she looked at Winifred's face she saw that she had been mistaken. Winifred had an apprehensive, almost miserable expression which she tried to chase away with the weakest of smiles, and Jessica knew that both of these women wanted to make their rich relative believe that they lived in a modestly beaming, all-sufficient world and were her equals in spite of the financial contrast. They couldn't see that equality was a matter of thought and feeling, and if she had displayed a mentality quicker and better informed than theirs they would not have been downcast, but they were ashamed of their material circumstances and anxiously resorted to an expression of babbling, proud contentment. Would she have been the same if she had been poor? A yes and a no rose within her and were unable to overcome each other.

She turned the conversation to other subjects. She found that Winifred had planned a series of teas, and suppers, and parties for her, and she shocked her aunt by declining these social arrangements.

"I'm trying to escape from that kind of a world," she said. "To be frank with you, the fewer human beings I see here the better. I've had too many of them lately and I want to be more alone with myself. I'll take my easel and paint in the park here, or walk about London, or take trips to the countryside. A formal affair of any kind would just about slay me now."

"I only wanted you to meet some very particular friends," answered Winifred, aggrievedly. "You'd like them, I know—they're all very jolly and decent."

"I can sympathize with cousin Jessica," said Ruth. "One does become so tired of this party and that dance, and it's much nicer to be alone with yourself sometimes and feel that you don't really *need* people."

She wanted to imitate Jessica's "social boredom" because she felt that no woman could seem to be important unless she professed to be very tired of the things around her now and then. It was necessary for her to be gleefully content with her material surroundings, but she must hint now and then that she was really destined for better people than those whom she had already met. After a half-hearted argument, the Swinsons gave in to Jessica's desire for seclusion. It would spare them a great deal of expense, and their friends could be told that a girl of Jessica's wealth and position could hardly be expected to be interested in ordinary gatherings and festivities.

Richard Swinson came in later, and asked Jessica questions concerning her father's business affairs, and strove to speak as one substantial business man referring to a distant partner in a general, commercial enterprise, and fingered the pink carnation on his coat as he twitted her about the men whom she would conquer in England. After the dinner, they all went to one of the Soho theaters and saw one of the politely almost risque, effervescent-about-nothing, ingenuous comedies that English audiences adore and American ones treat more fickly. It was all about a pair of green stockings owned by a Duchess but found in a servant girl's room in the chateau by the Duke himself, who had gone there for no intrinsically worthy purpose. The stockings proved to be an impetus which induced every one to accuse the other person of philandering, but every one finally established his innocence or escaped from the consequences of his airy lust, and, of course, the Duke discovered that his wife had not had an affair with the young gardener, as he had suspected. The play seemed to have been written by an intelligent butler, who had drawn upon his past experiences in the households of the nobility and was whimsically fawning upon his characters, and wittily amending their originally stupid remarks, to make them appear to be *charming people.*

Afterwards, as they rode home in a taxi-cab, Jessica discussed the play with the Swinsons.

"Thirty minutes of it might have been endurable, but two hours—impossible," she said. "When people act like neurotic babies in distress they're never humorous unless their mouths have been stuffed with the drollest of speeches, and even then . . . Besides, I don't like playwrights who kiss the feet of their people and then try to make you laugh, so you won't see what's happening."

"There was a great deal of kissing in the play, but I didn't see any one kissing any one else's feet," said Winifred. "I don't know what you mean."

"Oh, Jessica thinks that the Duke and the Duchess

were made to be much nicer than, well, than they would be in real life," Ruth said. "It's curious, the ideas that American people always have about Dukes and Duchesses. Even dear Jessica believes that they nev-er say anything clever, and walk around with the most horribly frozen faces. Of course, they're ever so much different."

"We don't worship our nobility, I should hope," said Winifred, "but we know that most of them are very delightful people, and very democratic. I remember the time, years ago, when I met the young Earl of Trevington, at a flower exhibition. He was so gracious, and yet so sincere, and you could tell that he didn't think he was at all better than you were."

"I've been to plays that made me laugh much more," said Richard, who wanted to side with his niece, because she was pretty and spoke to the effu-sive gallantry which his life had crushed within him, and because he had always felt that a noble birth might have given his intelligence a greater chance to exert itself. "I can't say that the moral examples set by our nobility are very inspiring ones, and they induce too many people to follow them. Our divorce courts are becoming more and more crowded every day."

"I'm prejudiced, of course, and I deserve to be sat on," answered Jessica, calmly. "I suppose it's all because I met a real Duke once at a ball in New York. He was middle aged, and he had the hardest time trying to be affable and dignified at the same time, without showing where one ended and the other commenced, and he had the sweetest of looks on his face. It seemed to whisper: 'I could say something very witty, if you would only stimulate me to it.' "

The Swinsons felt that Jessica was being desperately impudent to conceal her respect for the personage in question, and that they must be tolerant toward such youthful grimaces. During the next week, Jessica sat in the park at Tavistock Square and painted angular, bizarre versions of the trees, and flowers, and nursemaids, or strolled about the tortuous, musty, narrow streets leading off from Piccadilly Circus. The Swinsons, and her other relatives who dropped in to see her, bored her with their adulterated, unspiced emotions, and with the pallid ploddings of their thoughts. The women showered her with kindnesses and favors, to keep their envy of her from growing too self-conscious, and one of her distant cousins—a rosy, Wertherish young barrister—came to the Swinson home every night, and seemed to be immune to the strongest of rebuffs, and recited Wordsworth and Swinburne with the inference that he could have surpassed them if his mundane parents had not driven him into the graveyard of law, and pursued her without much hope but simply because one could not let a comely heiress vanish without some form of courtship.

After a week and a half had passed, Jessica rented a furnished apartment in Chelsea—one that over-looked the Thames Embankment—and told the Swinsons that she was leaving them because painters frequently had moods in which they wanted to be secluded and concentrate on their work, and think only of light, and color, and form—qualities which even the best of human beings sometimes obstructed. She hoped that they would not be vexed if she failed to give them her address, and she would come to see them regularly. The Swinsons gave her a hurt silence at first and then, against their will, they began to feel relieved. It made you uncomfortable to live with a relative who had so much more money than you had, even though she was a likable, unassuming creature, because the immediate contrast brought you a robbed and almost complaining spirit—to think of what you could have done with her advantages!— and because you had to waver constantly between accepting her gifts and proudly declining them, and because her presence caused you to spend far more than you could afford, in the effort to entertain and impress her. Besides, while they looked upon her painting as the whim of an idly wealthy girl, they were embarrassed at not being able to talk about it with her and having to admit that she was versed in a refined something that they were ignorant of.

On the third day after Jessica had moved into her apartment, she met a college chum whom she had not seen for several years, and who was visiting England. It happened on a bus going to Charing Cross, and she and the other girl acted in the effusive, unnaturally joyous way in which long-separated people greet each other when they have accidentally met in a foreign country. They may have practically forgotten each other, and may no longer be innately congenial, but in the first babbling of memories shared together, and in the desire to form an alliance against new surroundings, they take on a pleasant and faultless aspect. The other, Cecelia Burnham, was the plumpest bundle of a girl, with green eyes that were too large for her small face and gave it an ingenuously inquisitive look, and a stubby nose whose tininess prevented it from being ugly, and long, bright red hair, and a short body. She was sophisticated without being deep, and coquettish without being sexually experienced, and thoughtful without being creative, and in her entirety she was forever poised between callowness and an assumption of jaded insight, while both qualities joined to a third one that prattled indecisively and was capable of the greatest visions and the blindest perceptions. She worked as an interior decorator in a New York department store—one who showed recently rich people how to furnish their homes without indicating the newness of their financial rise—and she was having her customary three months' summer vacation from this position.

After she and Jessica had exhausted their college reminiscences, she mentioned a club of which she was a member and to which she was going for lunch. It was called the "1919 Club"—in commemoration of a Russian revolution—and it was composed of radical members of parliament, labor party people, artists, writers, social workers, and business men who were cultured without being conservative. Cecelia had become an honorary member of the club through an introduction given by a London artist whom she had met in New York, and she bubbled over with descriptions of the intelligent, informal atmosphere of the club.

"Of course, they all take themselves a little seriously—English people are never quite free from a kind of over-upright restraint, even at their best," she said, "but then they've all done things, or else they're trying to, so it's easy to excuse them."

"Has this paradise a few men who know how to talk about themselves without making you regret their egotism?" asked Jessica. "I've been meeting nothing but the other kind lately and it's forced me to become a recluse."

"Lately," said Cecelia, in mock surprise. "If you ever did meet them you're wonderfully lucky. They're in the singular form—one in a lifetime, Jes', and twice if you've got some secret arrangement with the gods. I met a girl once who claimed she had run across three men whose conversation was like—like borrowing wings, you know, and she said she couldn't decide between them, but I know she was fibbing just to upset me."

"I didn't want to admit that I was still waiting for the first one, but there *are* relative degrees," answered Jessica. "I don't usually get along well with women because they think I'm self-centered, you know, when I'm only trying to talk about something else besides frocks and trousers. Or else I'm not se-ri-ous enough for them because I don't do some kind of useless-useful work and help the starving children on Hester Street. Charity and investigation, you know, while nothing really changes. Do you know any men who can interest a woman for two hours at a time with their conversation, and then dance with her at the point where talking ought to end?"

"Most Englishmen don't dance," said Cecelia, mournfully. "They toddle, like something brisk but undecided, or they waddle like ducks on a spring, or they walk around just as though they were drilling in the army. I've met one, though, who's really not too bad. He can fox-trot without wrecking you, and he's logical but he doesn't issue any instructions on the subject. He's tall, and he'd be good-looking if it weren't for his large nose. Still, a nose can shrink a little when there are other attractions."

"What does this unique man do, when he isn't amazing some woman?" asked Jessica.

"He was a captain during the war and he's studying economics now at the government's expense," Cecelia answered. "Sort of an idea to make their former officers able to take commanding positions

in civil life and compensate them for their interrupted educations.   Something like our own voca-
tional bureau stuff, but without the graft and in-
competence."

"Are you making a play for him?" asked Jessica.

"I haven't a chance," Cecelia answered.   "I don't
quite come up to his shoulder, and that's always a
greater obstacle than it seems—you know what I
mean—and besides, I think a red-haired woman must
have jilted him once.   I remember, one day he said
that when a woman had red hair it made him forget
all about her face, which was unfortunate, because
the hair couldn't hear what he was silently saying
to it.   Imagine!"

"I'll refuse to believe that a consistently whimsical man exists until I meet him, but it does sound
promising," Jessica said.

"I'll introduce you to him at the club—he's a
member and his name's Robert Chamberlain," answered Cecelia.   "Find out for yourself."

They stepped from the omnibus and walked down
a narrow street that zigzagged away from one of
London's prominent theaters.   Cecelia's glances
slanted at Jessica's dress of dark red silk trimmed
with ermine fur at the top and bottom and having
that ingeniously saucy, softly expensive look that
proclaims Paris, and Jessica knew that Cecelia was
reverting back to her own plain, black satin gown
and probably hating Jessica for being rich enough
to wear such costly clothes.   Yet, Cecelia looked just

as debonair and appropriately clad as Jessica did. Why did women nearly always feel that the attractiveness of clothes was entirely a matter of their price? Jessica told herself that she paid a great deal for clothes merely because it would have been ridiculous to hang on to money when she had loads of it, and that she could have dressed just as well on figurative pennies. When a woman is accustomed to wealth but does not care to believe that it is her main rescue, she often goes to an extreme in deriding its favors and its value, and feels immensely unburdened about it.

They entered the club, which occupied a three-story, red brick house along the lane—it was little more than that—on which they had been walking. A restaurant was operated in the basement of the building, for members and their guests, where an excellent meal could be obtained for two and sixpence, and the upper stories had reading and lounging rooms, and alcoves where the members could talk to their friends in privacy. The furniture was of plain oak; there were no pictures on the yellow walls; and all of the place had a brightly stripped, unobtrusive air. After the luncheon, Cecelia and Jessica sat in one of the upper rooms and Cecelia identified some of the people walking in and out— people to whom she did not introduce Jessica because she knew them too slightly.

A tall, sturdy man came in, chatting to a prim wisp of a middle-aged woman who might have been his secretary. He had a blunt, heavily mustached face, a high, seared forehead below his gray-black hair, calmly fatigued eyes, and a nose that ended in a little knob. Afterwards, he was to become a temporarily supreme figure in the government of England.

"That man who just walked in—he's Ronald Mac-Lenard, a member of parliament and a labor leader," said Cecelia. "Isn't there something of an uninspired, kindly ox about him? I spoke to him once and it took him two minutes to say one, little sentence, and even then you knew he was afraid he hadn't considered the matter enough."

"I never judge people by their looks," answered Jessica. "I've made so many mistakes thinking that bricklayers were poets and artists were shoe clerks that I've given up in despair."

"Well, MacLenard is one of the few people whom you can't go wrong on," Cecelia answered. "You might not be able to tell that he was a member of parliament but you'd see immediately that he had politics and helping social conditions en-gra-a-aved all over him. They're always that way—heavy, and tired, and a little carelessly dressed, and trying so hard to be tolerant and reserved at the same time."

Jessica liked the flippantly assured manner in which Cecelia chattered on, and she felt relieved at listening to a woman whose mind had some degree of zest and inquiry. What did her sex ever seem to have in its head except sexual intrigues, or frothy banishings of thought, or lines taken from books and mussed up just enough to throw doubt on their origin, or weighty plans for improving the world, or cradled contentments?   Perhaps women could never be huge creators, save in those rare cases where they had a great deal of the masculine in them—a cheeky apology for herself, wasn't it? Within herself, what was the thing that enabled her to see other people's faults and lacks so clearly, while she herself could do nothing more than contemplate them? Was she reducing men and women to a pigmy size in order to avoid seeing her own smallness?   Fitfully, these thoughts came and went in the back spaces of her head as she listened to Cecelia's comments.

A pair of tall, young men entered the room and surveyed it with the most peculiar mien that Jessica had ever observed—a look of plaintive but self-contained, painfully erect, immaculately glowing boredom. Both of them were dressed in loose, gray suits, with spats to match, and the most scrupulously correct collars and cravats, and they carried silver-topped canes which hung from their lifted forearms. The stoutest and oldest of the two had a slightly florid face, with drooping, gray eyes, brown hair, and an outwardly curved nose, while the other was lean, with high cheek bones, darker hair, and a more solemn face. They sat down heavily and were motionless and seemed to be inspecting something on the bare walls that nobody else could see.

"Those two who just came in—they look like

aristocrats of a certain kind so they're probably bank clerks on a holiday," said Jessica.

"No, your hundred to one shot came home that time," answered Cecelia. "Their mother is Lady Sanville and their blood couldn't possibly be bluer, unless they were cousins to the king. The oldest one is Oliver Sanville and the other one's Senrin, his brother."

"Do they do anything else besides manipulate their canes and pray for amusement?" Jessica inquired.

"Yes, indeedy," said Cecelia. "They're both poets, and they've got a sister who's a poet too. I never heard of them before I came to England, but I understand that they have a large following over here. I bought two of their books a while ago and managed to get through them, after much suffering. Oliver writes political satires and grotesque exposures of the people in his own class, while Senrin sticks to the birdies and the hills at evening."

"Poetry's a blessing in one way," answered Jessica. "It gives so many people a chance to believe that they can sing without trying out before any stage manager or opera director."

"I don't know much about poetry," Cecelia confessed. "I like it when it tells me something I wanted to say myself but couldn't think of the right words for it. When I feel that I could say the thing just as well as the poet does then I don't believe he amounts to much, because I'm certainly not a poet myself!"

Another man in a brown suit sauntered in, and his bearing said: "We must be well acquainted before I recognize you, and even then . . ." He had a smoothly pale face beneath his black hair, and his eyes had a well-informed haughtiness about them, and his nose was prominent above thick, closed lips.

"That's James Myron Morton, editor of the *Coliseum,*" said Cecelia. "He always acts as though he were going to be of historical importance! He's a literary critic and I've been told he's very conservative but he pats some radical writer on the head now and then. You know, this is a terribly condescending country. Everybody seems to be unbending to the other person, with a kind of, oh, a kind of perfectly disguised contempt. I don't know any other way of expressing it."

"They've had so many centuries to make things run smoothly over here," answered Jessica. "They don't splash all over the place, the way we do, because they're a little nearer to knowing that it's futile to be happy or sad. Just a little nearer. I think it's this extra inch of knowledge that makes them more self-possessed on the surface, though at bottom they're just as emotional and foolish as we are."

"Maybe," Cecelia said, "but you'd never guess it to look at some of the people who come in here. If I ever saw any boisterousness or bluntness over here, except from low-brows on the street, I'd have a case of heart failure!"

"You'll live, don't worry," Jessica replied, smiling.

A woman of thirty, or a bit over, appeared, with a walk that was not girlish but approached it, with a hitch of the shoulders and a bold stride. She was dressed in a black, sleeveless gown and had curly, black, bobbed hair, and a round, vividly brown face with naturally red cheeks. She was of medium height, with an uncurved but plump body, and there was an abrupt, peasant-woman prettiness on her features."

"There goes my double—almost," said Jessica. "Who is she, Cel'? You seem to know every one here."

"She's Rachel Winton, the novelist. I've met her just long enough to say how-do-you-do and some more empty things, and she acts, well, I don't quite know what to call it. Merrily insolent, I suppose, though the two words don't go together. As though she knew more than you did but didn't want to hurt you about it. She writes realistic, talkative novels and she goes to America to lecture and captivates every one there, but she's not so frightfully popular over here, I understand."

"Our beloved country does like to bring candy to the visitors," said Jessica. "We're so horribly young and commercial, you know, and they simply must know more about art and life than we do—just like that."

A very tall, very thin, very pale man came in. He had a brown, clipped mustache, and a wave of brown hair brushed back over his head, and a young face that would have looked owlish if it had not been so diffident. His dark clothes were close to shabbiness but he wore them as though he were unclad.

"Who's the man standing beside the short one in the corner?" asked Jessica.

"That's Alvin Hurley, the writer. He's very daring and grotesque and ironical in his sex stuff, and he's always writing about perversions, and libertines, and naughty women. It's a funny conundrum, Jes'. Hurley's a married man, and he's faithful to his wife, and he lives the most conventional and humdrum of existences. Do they *always* write it as a kind of consolation?"

"Oh, I don't suppose there's any rule," Jessica replied, "but they hardly ever seem to write about anything that's happened to them, unless they want to make it more satisfying than it really is."

She continued to listen to Cecelia's jaunty, barely malicious descriptions of the people who passed in and out, and she knew that none of them were quite true, but what did that matter? Truth was the ability to lie a little more plausibly than any one else could—in your own opinion and in that of others —without your realizing it.

She and Cecelia went to a theater that night and

arranged to meet on the following noon, and Cecelia promised that she would bring Chamberlain if he were not engaged. Neither of the women was certain of how much she liked the other, but they were grateful for the fact that they had a number of similar interests and could talk about them without becoming annoyed or disagreeable. They had been surfeited with women to whom art was a piece of costly confectionery, and to whom men were subjects of worship, or plundering, and they were glad to be able to talk to each other more freely than they could to other women. Underneath all of this, their respective emotions were carefully watching each other and wondering whether they ought to be jealous, or receptive. Envying Cecelia's material independence, Jessica reflected on whether she herself had not missed a superb thrill—the thrill of earning your own money and fretting or being pleased about it, so that it meant something to you—instead of taking checks and spending large sums, with no emotion. How could any one be happy when there was so little to be fought for, and cried about, and renounced, unless they were overpoweringly physical, or so creatively abstracted that they hardly ever lived in the world of flesh and comforts? If you were poor, you went without numbers of things, but it taught you to exaggerate the value of the things that you were able to win, and it kept you from moodily drifting through your days. She had never had the sense of struggling, and breathing hard, and knocking her head against every kind of wall, and perhaps this was why her painting had never expanded as it should have done. If she had been poor at the start, and had afterwards acquired wealth, she might still have progressed, but you had to be beaten around at least once in your lifetime before you could make yourself strong and articulate. She played again with the idea of cutting herself off from her father's money and earning her own way, but when she began to visualize the daily details that would come with such a change, her spirit became shrinking and still. A drab uninviting room; unvaried and untempting food; riding in crowded, suffocating tramways; theaters, dances, and concerts reduced to a minimum, unless you were willing to accept the company of obnoxious men—no, it was a dream that looked uglier and much less stimulating when you viewed it closely. Enduring such things had to be pounded into you for years—you couldn't suddenly embrace them without wrenching and stunning your spirit.

Cecelia, on her part, looked upon Jessica's life as a ravishing abundance of luxuries, and leisures, and opportunities, and felt that she could never be actually friendly with Jessica because a sense of unfairness would cause her, Cecelia, to look eagerly for flaws and faults in the other woman. Somehow, you couldn't separate a person from her money, and it made her either a comrade or one who was able to stand unjustly above you. She had saved for

over a year to take this summer trip—part of her
salary of one hundred dollars a week went toward
the support of a mother and sister—while Jessica
had probably become bored with New York one
morning and had immediately purchased her passage! When they had gone to college together, the
similarity of studies and dormitory rooms, and a
dashing, flapperish simplicity of clothes had taken the
bitter edge from Jessica's wealth, but now it was an
obviously flaunted thing, and the old, exuberant comradeship had fled.

Again, through instinct and the less daunted eye
which women give each other, Cecelia sensed that
Jessica had been possessed by several men. Cecelia
herself was an almost-virgin, having had but one,
full experience where the man had subsequently jilted
her and left an even more frightened soreness in
her heart. She regarded sex as a cruel, half-mysteri-
ous devourer, where women gave everything and
men offered nothing but a few hours of their fickle
and untouched emotions, and she never allowed the
caresses of men to subdue her. Her system was to
become indirectly gratified without actually yielding
herself, not because she was sly and calculating but
because the shadow of the first man always intruded
at the crucial moment and kept her from abandoning herself. She was waiting for a man who would
be handsome, mentally intriguing, and anxious to
marry her—he could be as poor as the lowest of
vagabonds, she didn't care about that—and each of

the men that she had met had always been lacking in at least one of these three essentials. She was piqued at the thought that Jessica had carelessly taken the pleasures of sex—when you were rich it even helped you sexually, because you could meet so many different kinds of men and give most of your time to examining them—and this made it impossible for her to act quite spontaneously in Jessica's presence.

Robert Chamberlain was out of town, and for two weeks Cecelia and Jessica scampered around London and its suburbs, from studios to country houses. Jessica met creators and people of the artistic middle classes, and always found them to be shallow and over-rigid after a second meeting. They were at their best when they were first speaking to her, as though they had carefully dressed up then, and had been surprised in their negligée at a second meeting. The one respect in which they seemed to differ from their prototypes in America was in suaver and more measured tricks of speech and posture, and in a tendency to look down more often than up without letting the attitude become too apparent! Jessica hunted in vain for the pale, dark-eyed, cleverly neurasthenic men and women whom she had read so much about on the pages of the younger English novelists, and she humorously said to herself that they must have lived and died exclusively in the brains of the men and women who wrote about them. Even the droll, flagrant bounders turned out to be men with strong ambitions and fumbling tactics. When a bouncing, chipper young man sought to do more than kiss her, as they sat in his studio, she grew bewildered and asked him how long he had lived in England. Meeting people is a staggering gamble, and you may always run across the same general kind for one year, or seven different kinds in a single day.

When Chamberlain returned, she met him at a dinner in the "1919 Club," in the company of Cecelia and a Jewish real-estate broker named Joseph Israel. In her descriptions of Chamberlain, Cecelia had voiced many eulogies, disparagements repentantly trailing off into rhapsodies, and assertions of indifference, and Jessica guessed that Cecelia might be in the forlorn turmoil of a woman toward a man who had not responded to her emotions. In reality, Cecelia had long since given up hope of capturing Chamberlain and was nervously setting herself in order after the tumult that she had had, not caring to dismiss him too instantly or to infer that he had not been worthy of her past feelings. She would never consent to become the mistress of any man— even the best one—and men would never have a chance to gloat over her accessibility and then turn away (she still told herself that she had rejected the first man and that he had not really spurned her).

Fearing that she might hurt her friend, Jessica strove to be genially attentive to Chamberlain without definitely responding to him, but he had a man-

ner of taking you into his confidence without seeming
to be presumptuous or hasty, if you interested him,
and his wit was too graceful and unconcerned for
your coldness to hold out against him. He was the
kind of man who had scores of friends who were not
really friends, and no enemies but people who
vaguely distrusted him because they felt that he was
always adjusting his opinions to those of the person
in front of him. Men spoke well of him but had no
deeper reactions, and would never have rushed to his
side in a moment of trouble, and women either loved
him or spoke of him as a clever but impossible jester.
He was tall and too slender for his height, but he
carried himself with a straightness that made him
seem much stronger than he was. The sharp hook
of his nose, his high forehead rising to curly, brown
hair, and widely sensitive lips, were gathered to the
self-suspicious look of an ordinary intelligence that
used humor to escape from its own naïvetés.

As the party lingered over its wine in the restaurant of the club, he began to banter with Jessica on
the subject of sex.

"Have you heard about the latest school in sexology?" he asked.

"I never dream much, except when I'm awake, so
don't tell me about it," answered Jessica. "If you're
very careful about what you eat, and when you eat it,
you can avoid having people tell you that you're
hungry in a different way. Sleeping on your right

side and not on your back is another great help, I've found."

"I haven't had an insult as bad as that in months —expecting me to talk about Freud," Chamberlain said. "He passed out when the first crop of starved men and women became less starved and less anxious, as they naturally would after following his theories. The present crop is looking for a less simple explanation. Sex, you know, is a very simple matter, and it would lose its charm if people didn't invent complicated doubts and theories about it."

"Well, what *is* this latest school?" asked Israel, a small, lean man with black hair and a coldly sad face that barely relaxed when he was amused. "If it is going to be a pun, or a few paradoxical adjectives, I'll shun you for the rest of my days!"

"These slanderous conceptions of my intelligence are beginning to irritate me," said Chamberlain, smiling. "The latest school in sexology is an excellent compromise. They admit that we have a soul, and a mind that can function independently—all of that, you know—but they insist that sex was provided as an entertainment for this mind and soul. They claim that without sex the mind and soul would grow disconsolate, you see, and would lament the lack of competition—sort of like wandering through the Soho district with all of the theaters and restaurants closed, and not caring to go home so early. Their idea is to look upon sex as a condition where you can laugh, or be gorgeously dramatic, and then trot off to your more serious work, knowing all the time that your thoughts and your spirit have not really been affected."

"It seems to me that most people have been making this practical compromise for hundreds of years," answered Israel.

"Yes, but they've always been mawkishly repentant, or brazen, or muddled about it," Chamberlain said. "They've always been afraid that they were doing wrong and that their souls and minds were involved in the wrongness. They've never made a theory that could put the matter on a clear and confident basis. This new school does away with all of the old qualms and quandaries, and we can certainly accomplish more when we know that sex is, well, is only the violent servant that we've hired for purposes of recreation."

"It's not a bad idea, considering the fact that you've probably made it up during the past five minutes," Jessica said. "You might simply have said—divide yourself into pagan and ascetic and try not to feel too hypocritical about it. That's what most men and women do, unless they're positively hoggish. Of course, it might be nice if they could pay the pagan a salary and put him in his place, without really disturbing his intentions!"

"It might be difficult to fix the right price," Israel said, with one of his chill approaches to a smile.

"How can all of you talk so lightly about something that's forever haunting you?" asked Cecelia.

"You all try to dismiss the bogie-man by grinning at him! Everyone's always laughing about sex, or denouncing it, and I don't know which is worse."

"My dear Cecelia, we can't be serious about something that's entirely too serious itself," Israel answered. "The strain would be tremendous, and unprofitable in the bargain!"

The party adjourned to Israel's apartment, where the chaffing continued over bottles of Tokay. Cecelia became nonchalantly tipsy and retired to a sofa with Israel, where they embraced as though they were tentatively luring each other on, and declaimed passages from Swinburne and Dowson, and wondered whether they would become reckless enough to forget the other couple. Jessica and Chamberlain sat together and drank their wine with an increasing silence. Silence, thought Jessica, was a dangerous interval, colored and molded by the words that had already been spoken and the words that were yet to be uttered, and it was the only way in which you could find out how much you liked a person. When you were talking with him, he could deceive you and make you believe that you were more pleased or averse than you really were, but when you were both silent together you judged his words more slowly and came to firmer conclusions. When the silence ratified your previous sensations and responses, you liked the other person, and when it did not, you felt that he had been playing a part and that you would have to search for his more actual self. When the silence was merely an empty one, occurring because neither of you could think of anything more to say to each other, you knew that you were both alien people who had vainly striven to become harmonious.

As she sat beside Chamberlain she felt that they were both withholding words because they wanted to test each other's ability at divining what the words would have been—a warm, loosely acceptant feeling. She liked Chamberlain's whimsical sentences, and was glad that he could become silent at the time when whimsicality always grows a little thin and worn from much utterance, and when seriousness would have been a blundering intrusion. This habit that people always had of fearing that prolonged silence would make them stupid or tiresome—it caused them to ruin the interest that needed a more miserly nursing!

To Chamberlain, Jessica was one of the most desirable girls that he had ever met—sophisticated without being haughty, girlish and old-womanish in a quickly shifting way that made both qualities seem unreal, and physically beautiful in a semi-voluptuous manner, with the other half sedately adolescent—a beauty that he had always longed for and observed only at a distance. And the novelty of meeting a woman who had a brain but did not force it upon you on all occasions—he had almost forgotten that such women existed. He had a feeling that the usual, confident approaches would never serve in

Jessica's case, and that a surprised tenderness might rise within her if he courted her patiently, without the slightest attempt at physical embraces. He guessed that she was far from being a virgin, and might be craving the interlude of a warmly poised friendship with a man. They would run about together, and talk, and be comrades to each other, and then, when the appropriate moment came without warning or reason, as it always does, she would abruptly discover her emotions and feel the futility of denying them any further and he would be repaid for all of his restraints. The thought of this finale weakened him, as he looked at Jessica's diminutively chiseled, abstracted, whitish brown face and the half-ripe curves of her body, and he was about to touch her but controlled himself and felt self-congratulatory. He could show her now that even under the influence of wine he was not the determined, undressed animal that most men became in their cups.

Shortly after midnight Cecelia rose unsteadily from the couch, where she and Israel had been reclining intimately but not perilously, and walked over to shake Jessica's shoulder.

"Wake up—dummies," she cried, gayly. "Joseph's going to take us to the Trafalgar Dancing Club. It's not supposed to be open at this hour, you know, but you can get in if you're with some one who's extra-or-dinarily well known, and Joseph is posi-lively——no, -tively notorious! That sounded funny when it came out, but it's true!"

"I don't think that Miss Maringold cares to dance," said Chamberlain. "Certain kinds of silences, you know, are more exhausting than hours of talking, and so we're both rather tired while you and Israel are as fresh as daisies in the moon."

Jessica saluted him inwardly—a man who could discern your mood without your announcing it to him through a figurative megaphone! She would have to give an extended investigation to this deliciously weird gentleman.

"So you've gone to the moon and picked daisies there," said Cecelia, who craved to make an impertinently nonsensical remark. "Is there anything you haven't done?"

"Yes, I've never been able to bring them back to the earth, but naturally they always wilt in a more substantial place," Chamberlain answered, not quite knowing the meaning of his own words but voicing a hazily, delicately sentimental mood.

"Well, come and dance with us and forget your horticultural aspirations," said Israel. "Both of you are acting like impossible children. A mood can always be changed in a moment's notice, and yet we tell ourselves that it can't because we like to feel sad and helpless about it."

"I don't want to ruin the party but wine always makes me sleepy," Jessica replied, "and when your mind just persists in working, in spite of your sleepiness, then a fox-trot would be absolutely ludicrous. You'd never be aware that you were dancing it!"

Israel believed that Jessica and Chamberlain were both dodging the dance club because they wanted to be alone with each other, and he ended his urging. The party separated into taxi-cabs and Chamberlain and Jessica went to her apartment. Jessica did not even ask him to step in—it seemed natural to both of them that they should resume the conversation which had been interrupted by the paying of the taxi-cab driver. The usual parleying, and asking without appearing to ask, and suggested terminations, which occur between a man and woman who have not arranged for a rendezvous but are facing the prospect of one, were not spoken by Jessica and Chamberlain because their desire to remain with each other was a warmly obvious one. They sat in the parlor of her apartment and talked about different authors—Havelock Ellis, Moore, and an American poet famous for his rough colloquialisms on men who toil with their hands, and an English apostle of mincing, cerise decadence—and during the course of the talk Jessica partly unloosened her heliotrope blouse because of the warmness of the room, and sprawled at ease on a couch without a thought of sensual invitation. Intent upon impressing her with his ideas and word-frolics Chamberlain forgot the inference of the scene for a time, but when Jessica happened to bend over to light a cigarette, and he saw the softly full, ivory-shadowed, impalpably smooth division of her breast underneath the blouse, he winced, as though he had been pitilessly goaded and could no longer stay in his chair. Human beings—how many thousands of reasons and situations were constantly interfering with the simple contacts for which men and women had been intended! It would be easy to walk over to her now and grasp her, yet she would probably resist him, wearily, or hate him afterwards for having disrupted her intangible mood. It was almost as though Nature and an outside, mystic Devil, were endlessly warring with each other. Yes, afraid to be happy for more than a moment, and lacking the ability to be happy for a longer period, human beings often coldly or unwittingly used each other for purposes of subtle revenge.

His confidently thoughtful mood was shattered, and for the first time he looked steadily at the tapering, disciplined curves of her legs, slowly losing their plumpness as their lines fell to her ankles, and half revealed by her raised, white skirt; and the sloping narrowness of her shoulders, and her small-lipped, impishly not quite round face that was glinting and tenuous in the moderated light of the room. He was about to rise from the chair and risk everything in one appeal when he heard her saying: "I'm very tired now and I'm going to bed. You won't be angry, will you?"

The cool stress of her voice, showing that she was unaware of his torments, or unresponsive, steadied him.   In another woman, he might have fancied that she was plaguing him to see what he would do, and she would remain indecisive until he made a plain overture, but he felt that Jessica's calmness was genuine.   You never really knew about such things, and you had to rely upon—well, call it instinct, or an unwonted fear, or the subtlety of perceptions transcending themselves. She was tired of quick caresses, and the "love" that became a fleeting convenience when dawn returned, and she wanted to feel that at least one man could seek her for her thoughts and emotions alone—the old, wistfully engaging lie. He held her hand a moment and departed, after having arranged to see her at the end of the week.

Just before his departure she had wondered whether he would become amorous. The old situation: "Well, we've had an entire evening of talking because we didn't want to make the thing too precipitate or clumsy, but you're a woman and I'm a man and there's no escaping from *that,* sister!" After he had gone she felt lonely and perturbed. She had been over-cruel to him—she might have suggested that he could kiss her good-night. But kisses were always beginnings or ends—they didn't rest content with themselves. Again, her vanity might be running away with her—a habit which it often had. Perhaps he hadn't wanted to touch her—perhaps he had been lost in her own calm reveries. It was also possible that he might have controlled himself in the end, in the fear that she would think that he had been verbally dilly-dallying before trying to possess her. Suppose he had? The fact that a man could hold himself back indicated that his emotions might not be entirely physical, for otherwise his feelings often triumphed over his cautions. Yes, Chamberlain was a dear, unusual, delectably witty boy, and he might be the one that she had always sought but never found.

During the next two months she saw Chamberlain with an increasing frequency, until at last they were together almost every other day. They went to the theaters, and the races, or strolled around Hempstead Heath, like a giggling shop girl and her attentive but respectful suitor, or visited an aunt of his who lived in a cottage at Mitcham—a village just outside of London—where they walked down the orderly, neatly hedged roads and debated about music and poetry. Chamberlain clung to his physical aloofness because he felt that she had grown to expect it of him and that she would be unpleasantly disturbed if he dropped it. He could see no change in her own attitude—none of the lingering hands, or conscious shoulder-brushings, or heightened pressures during a dance, or reproachful glances with which a woman asks a man to interpret her signals without openly confessing that she has made them. He became more and more certain that she was reveling in a buoyant, peaceful friendship—with a tingle of motherly emotion in it—which she had never been able to have with any other man, and the conviction placed him on his mettle and made him averse to disrupting her singular dream. He was also sure that the first, visible recognition of sexual emotions would have to come from her, and that unless she could spontaneously rise to meet his love, of her own accord, she would always feel that he had broken something indelibly precious and had rudely tumbled their relations back to an earthly plane. It would be necessary for her to make her own discovery and to hold out her hands to him with an incredulous or humble swiftness and with the pathetic dread of one who feels that she may have lost something through ignoring it too long. Then he could bend down to her, with all of his pride healed and garlanded! Then they would take each other with that simultaneous, sweetly insane impatience without which love was never more than an empty tumult, or a heavily cheated game.

On her part, Jessica was charmed, and puzzled, and reflective. She did not know whether Chamberlain was physically unaffected by her or whether he was anxious to avoid sexual contact because he had too often rushed into it at the expense of a more lasting friendship, or whether he was binding himself because he wanted to be assured that her emotions were receptive. When she thought that the first explanation was true she felt piqued and pensive and said to herself: "How do you like *this* retribution, old girl?" When she believed that the second one was true she became determined to emu-

late his balance and foresight—wasn't this what she
had always wanted?—and when the third one seemed
to obtain she hesitated because she was not certain
that he had any physical appeal to her. He was humorous, and intellectual without being dogmatic—
eighth wonder of the world!—and he could be both
juvenile and mature without leaving an impression
of incongruity behind, but those things were, also,
not guarantees of physical desire and abandonment.
You never knew whether you loved a man until the
final moment of physical contact. Love had an il-
logical, heedless, potent fraction within itself that
accepted or spurned the arms of a man without telling you why, and refused to care whether he was a
fool or a sage. When this fraction was present, to
the exclusion of more tangible and more mental ones,
you were overpowered for a short time and then
dismally unsatisfied, and when it alone was absent,
you censured yourself for not loving the man and
tried in every way to simulate the missing something,
and you were depressed and unfulfilled. If she
loved Chamberlain, how could she have endured the
lack of his lips and breast? She was able to talk to
him and be with him without longing for his embraces, and she felt for him at different times a
tranquil admiration, or a sprightly communion, without being sensually aroused. As far as she could
discern, if he had been a woman, her reactions would
have been the same, except that no questions of uncertainty or future love would have occurred to her.

One of Chamberlain's uncles died, and he had to go to Liverpool and remain there a week to attend the funeral and take care of various legal formalities, since he was one of the heirs of the dead man's estate.   During his absence Jessica divided herself between painting and aimless pleasures, and placidly missed him without feeling any sharp loneliness. He had become an agreeable fixture in her mind and she had the feeling that she would always retain him, regardless of whether she saw him again in the flesh.   They had spoken about so many things, and she knew all of his eccentricities of thought and speech, and what else was left except to go over these things with newer words and more warmly practiced responses?   You could never really lose a comrade because he gave you qualities that could be perfectly restored in your memory, and his absent body was not a deterring influence.   It was probably true that she had failed to love him, but this would never be quite confirmed without the touch of his face, and hands, and breast.   It was possible that a first embrace with him might alter her in a second and flagellate her sleeping emotions, and give her the feeling that she had idiotically ignored the most insistently simple of requests within her heart.   Did human beings ever know themselves unless they tried to give freely of things that were either dead or alive? An electric wire—even one within yourself—meant nothing to you until you pressed a finger upon it! Chamberlain had been a dear, patient, stimulating man, and out of fairness to him she would invite him to make love to her, and find out once and for all whether she really desired him or not.

Her mood had come to this culmination one afternoon, as she sat in the "1919 Club" with Cecelia and a young actor named Caswell. Cecelia had deserted Israel because one night he had insisted upon finalities, and had told her that it would be best for them not to meet again unless she gave herself to him. He had gone on to say that he did not believe in marriage because one marriage and a subsequent divorce, in his past life, had convinced him that love needed to be free and voluntary, with no obligations save those made by its own impulses. He loved Cecelia—for as much as the word was worth—but he was forced honestly to admit that it might only last for a month, or a year, and he did not want to risk a marriage that might resolve into the quarrelsome or stoical farce which he had observed in so many other couples.

After arguing with him and asserting that marriage was a test of whether people felt a deep love, or a mere, passing lust for each other, Cecelia had wept and complained that all men were masked animals, with no real soul or heart within them. Israel had never quickened her blood and had never caused the major part of life to shrink within his outlines, but he was not physically repulsive to her, and she liked his briskly cynical spirit that was never quite practical and never quite illusioned. Ah, if he could

only be cynical to other people and obediently solici-
tous to her! She had set her heart upon marrying
him because she had felt certain that he was the best
man that she could possibly obtain, and now the old
situation had returned. Another man wanted to
drain her and walk over her, this time with bold
protestations of honesty and fairness, and then stroll
off to his next mistress, with an apologetic smile and
an unmarked heart! But suppose she were to love
a man again and then stop caring for him, while his
own affection remained? In that case she would be
willing to stifle her feelings and never leave the man,
unless she were utterly convinced that he loved someone else—what would life be if every one avoided
responsibilities and kindly burdens, and did nothing
but wound everyone else? An inexpressible nightmare!

Mistaking her weeping for an admission that she
could not resist him but desired to hold out until
the last moment, to spare her pride, Israel had
struggled with her until she was panting and half-
unclad, with her face piteously distorted and her
voice forever pleading with him to release her.
Then she had relaxed and said to him, in the coldest
of whispers: "You can have me, if this is the kind
of yielding you want, but I'll hate you for the rest of
my days, and you'll never, never see me again."
Abruptly, Israel had known that she was not acting
but was really a frightened, fettered, beclouded child
beneath all of her verbal sophistications. If he

took her it would be without any great relish and merely because of the stubborn momentum which his struggling had given to his sexual desires. Even if she had not literally meant her whispered threat, she would cling to him afterwards and act melodramatically at the slightest sign of infidelity on his part. His emotions toward her were sensual ones, tempered by a moderate regard for the æsthetic side of her nature, but he was by no means infatuated with her. If he lived with her, and then departed, she might strike at him viciously, heart-brokenly, as grown-up children always did. He looked down at her loosely cowering face, and the quick rise and fall of her bare, pinkish white, half curved breasts. He sighed, and gently buttoned her waist to cover her breast, lest the continued sight of it should sweep away his resolutions.

"You are right—I would only mar you and leave you with a cup of poison," he said. "You have no courage and you should never let life fling itself against you."

Afterwards, Cecelia had passed into a mood of hopeless composure. Since she had not loved him but had only reached for a refuge that had not materialized, her emotions could devise the balm of telling themselves that they were honorable and misunderstood in the midst of a carnally deceitful world. Then she had met Caswell—a youth whose masculinity was a doubtful equation—and had enjoyed the idea of running about with a safe companion for a change—one who paid compliments to her mind and "soul" without noticing or caring for her sex. Perhaps it would be wise to marry a man of this sort and forget sex for the rest of her life, and feel toward him as she would toward some dependent girl-baby.

As Jessica sat in one of the club parlors with Cecelia and Caswell, she listened to the latter with a tolerant ennui. Effeminate men always made her feel indulgent and unmoved—they were such exquisitely helpless travesties upon both sexes, and one might have liked them if they had not always insisted on talking too much. Caswell, a slender youth with much yellow hair and a brightly petulant, thin-featured face, was raving about a male æsthetic dancer whose feet were "swifter than hyacinths counting the heart-beats of a breeze"—he had read the line somewhere—while Cecelia nodded ecstatically and urged him on. Glancing toward the door, Jessica's eyes dilated a bit. Salburg was standing there and looking around the room.

When he saw her, he walked over with a surprised, uncertain greeting and she felt bothered and disarmed. Had he really pursued her to England—like the hero in one of those machine-made, popular novels? It was troublesome to meet a man to whom you had once given yourself and then completely forgotten—something like colliding with the wraith of a past human being and wondering how you should feel toward it and whether it would become solid again. Salburg explained that he had heard of her departure for Europe but had not known that she was in England, and had merely stopped off in London on his way to Paris, to give an exhibition of his paintings. An artist friend had taken him to the "1919 Club" two days previous, and he had been looking for the man when he spied Jessica.

After they had traded trivial observations about England and London, Salburg leaned toward Jessica and said in a low voice: "I must talk to you alone, if it's only for half an hour. I'm leaving England at the end of the week, and I'll promise not to bother you again, but you must let me talk to you now. Don't be enormously cruel about something that means much to me and nothing to you."

Jessica hesitated and then assented. She had not been overkind to this man, and he was only asking for a "morsel," but it would be a vaguely troublesome hour and she must take care not to let her pity lead her astray. They rode to her apartment and sat there for a while, in the most ponderous of silences.

"I want to explain to you why I am a coward," Salburg said, at last. "When I was a boy, about ten, I had a brutal governess who pummeled me with her fists, and tortured me whenever she could. I had caught her in a room with my father once and she wanted to frighten me into silence. It was useless to protest to my mother because the governess denied it, and invented terrible crimes and said that I

had committed them, and her word was believed
against mine. My mother was a dear, weakly, smiling, credulous woman, and my father cared little
for his children. An aversion to pain grew up within
me—a feeling that it could only be surmounted by
sneaking retreats, and whimperings, and lies of one
kind or another. The spirit of a child is a fragilely
appealing thing, easily nourished and easily trampled
upon. . . . Afterwards, when I had grown up, I
tried in every way to kill this cowardice, but it was
useless. Blows upon my face, blows upon my body,
they would make me shriek inwardly and step back
against my will, as though some outside force had
tied a string to my body and were jerking it! I am
being honest with you now, Jessica, without any hope,
of course, and only for the relief that it gives me."

Jessica listened to him with a maternal indecision
—how could she comfort this man, and what could
she give him except her body, which would only
be a tantalizing moment to him? Understanding?
But that never aided human beings unless it was
persistently attentive, and unmutilated, and respectful, and hers was not of that kind.

"I don't think you're a coward and it wouldn't
matter to me if you were," she answered, softly. "I
do think, though, that you have more of the feminine
than the masculine in your nature—just a little more
—but you've learned to masquerade so thoroughly,
even to yourself, that the feminine part never comes
out except in a time of physical danger. Your early

life must simply have encouraged something that was always in you, something that *wanted* to be encouraged. I've a feeling that people never yield to their environment unless there's something in these people that overwhelmingly responds. You were born with a delicate spirit, a spirit that could be easily distressed and bruised, and you weren't made for the roughness and rancors in this life of ours. You put on every kind of firmness and swagger because you've simply got to deceive yourself most of the time, in order to live. I can understand that. I don't love you, Kurt, and I don't love Purrel either. I can only love a man who's delicate and strong at the same time—that's the way I'm made. I haven't the least dislike for you, though. You must believe *that*."

"And if I didn't believe you, what would it matter?" he asked, wearily.

"I simply want you to know that I'm not silly enough to dislike a man merely because he can't swing his fists at other men," she said. "I don't see a reason on earth why we can't be friends with each other."

"If friendship means an empty tolerance to you, yes," he replied in the same weary voice. "It would be more invigorating if you detested me."

"Then I can't help you out—I don't," she said. "It's ridiculous to say that human beings can't have a calm, mild sort of feeling for each other.

They needn't always love, or hate, or just ignore each other."

"If you are kind to me before I leave England it may make me hate myself a little less," he answered, listlessly.

They turned the talk to impersonal subjects, and then returned to the club, where Cecelia, who had parted with Caswell, was waiting for Jessica. Jessica, who knew that Cecelia was a perturbed near-virgin, had a quizzical whim to bring Salburg and her friend together. Salburg might be able to capture Cecelia and give her a much-needed experience, and at any rate it would be interesting to see the outcome between such widely varying persons. She had an engagement for the evening and left both of them together at the club, with Cecelia prattling about French futuristic painters and Salburg looking resigned and trying to be genial. She did not see either of them until the end of the week, just before Chamberlain's scheduled return.

When they walked into one of the club-rooms, on a Saturday night, she noticed that they were holding hands and had a look of abashed, seraphic contentment on their faces. So Salburg had succeeded where fifty others had failed—he had an even greater cleverness than she had ever given him credit for. Or perhaps Cecelia's resistance had gradually become so feeble that she had determined to yield to the next, presentable, "artistic" man, no matter who he was.

They walked up to Jessica and stood like dreamy, nervous urchins.

"Well, we've done it," said Salburg.

"Done what?" asked Jessica.

"We were married this morning," Salburg answered. "We decided that marriage was an inevitable pit and that you might as well fall into it while you were still young instead of waiting for middle age. Besides, marriage is nothing in itself, nothing, and whether you turn it into a prison or into a garden is entirely up to you. We're going on to Paris next week and send for Cecelia's mother later on. We both feel very happy about it, and you can be as skeptical as you please—it won't matter to us."

"Kurt's going to make an artist out of me," said Cecelia, raptly. "I've always wanted to be one and I only needed some one to shove me along."

As Jessica congratulated them she felt amused, and sympathetic, and the least shade chagrined. She had been a conventional matchmaker when she had only intended to promote a flitting affair—a jovial experience. Again, while she was far from loving Salburg, it was not entirely comforting to see another girl whisk him away in a few days, while she, Jessica, had never been able to inspire him to any proposals of marriage! Still, it was deliciously absurd to feel annoyed because another woman had taken a man from whom you had fled. Cecelia was a woman who might really last as

Salburg's wife—one whose talkative adorations would give him a chance to believe that he was twice as intelligent and creative as he actually was. Marriage—would she be able to avoid it herself? It was a prosaic, weighty, convenient ending, and it said to you: "You're a creature of flesh, shaped in a certain way, and you must bind yourself forever to a differently shaped creature because you have only to choose between a safe and a dangerous emptiness, and because the dangerous one would eventually lose its quality of risk anyway, and because, after marriage, you can still flirt with clever men and be protected, and because you want to avenge yourself with children."

She felt sad, and dwindled, and swindled, as she listened to the plannings and endearments that passed between Salburg and Cecelia. Salburg had married Cecelia because he had become weary of the anticlimaxes, and blows, and distastes that came with one flirtation or another, and wanted to cling to this comely, worshiping woman, whose mind was assimilative but not as swift as his own. In addition, he could show Jessica that she had merely scratched him instead of inflicting any mortal wound, and thus lower her egotism! To Cecelia, Salburg was a genius, and a burnished man of the world, but a bruised child underneath all of his suaveness, and his offer of marriage had been ravishing to her. At last she could escape from the cruel designs of life and abandon herself without fear or punishment.

When Chamberlain came back, on the next day, Jessica met him at the station, and they went to his apartment on one of the side streets leading from Regent's Park. It was an intimately reposing place, all in grays, and blacks, and mauves, and even the prints and originals on the walls were black and white, or neutral-colored. Chamberlain was afraid of color because it jibed at all of the repressions and omissions of his life and gave him a feeling of floundering rebellion, and made him aware that he was not a poet but had always longed to be one. As he sat beside Jessica he felt humorously discontented and indiscreet, as though his painful longings were no longer impressive but had become an infinitely teasing jest, and he wanted to take Jessica in his arms, laughingly, and say: "Isn't it time that we stopped being ridiculous, and doubtful, and took the small pleasure that life has to offer us?"

To control himself, he talked about books and their makers, in a paradoxical fashion that might have been termed blithely jaded, and turned the leaves of a book which he had purchased before coming back to London.

"Listen to this," he said. " 'That exquisitely asinine blare which is England's punishment for having lost America'—the author is referring to your jazz music, of course, or thinks he is. Why is it that none of my countrymen, and nobody who lives over here, can mention anything American without becoming disparaging? This chap does it with a neat wit, but still, it's there."

"That's from 'Delightful People,' isn't it?" asked Jessica, as Chamberlain nodded. "I've read the book so I'll answer your conundrum, dear. They don't want to believe that the lit-tle boy has done something important which his father could never dream of doing. He simply must be verbally spanked, ever so lightly perhaps, but spanked just the same. Jazz music is really a deep, barbaric and original cry. It's 'a fatalist strutting-about with an insane, sad admiration of flesh'——the line isn't mine but it's true just the same. When he writes about jazz, though, the dear gentleman who lives in England simply must purse up his lips and twitter: 'Exquisitely asinine bl-a-are.' He likes it, of course, in a sneaking way, but he's peeved because England didn't invent it, that's all."

"Well, I don't know that that's any worse than the way you Americans go down on your knees in front of anything and everything that comes from England," said Chamberlain, smiling. "There isn't a third rate novelist here who can't go over to your country and come back with his pockets jingling with gold! Our veiled animosity, or whatever you want to call it, is much more interesting, even at its worst."

They carried on the subject a while longer, to

lull their feeling that a climax was impending between them. They were like people whose bodies had suddenly become naked to each other, trying to converse about the weather to hide their exposures. Then Chamberlain rose and sat beside her on the low bed that was disguised as a couch, with a black silk cover that touched the floor, and several, small, gray cushions.

"I love you," he said, slowly. "It's easier to say it without adornment, as a helpless school boy would, because that's what it makes you anyway. I've said nothing of this before because, well, because instant claims of love always sound false and meaningless. And there was another reason. I felt that you were tired of sensual things, always leaping upon you without warning, without preparation, as though there were nothing else in life. I wanted to give you a friendship that no other man might have given you—I wanted to show you that you were not just another pretty woman to me. But now, all of it seems wasteful, and unbearable, and ludicrous to me. A time comes when restraint loses its value and then it changes to fear and emptiness."

Jessica listened to him with a confusion of emotions that changed in the lapse of a few seconds and came back in the same space of time—hopelessness, doubt, admiration, compassion, self-reproach, and sadness, all of them struggling for her heart. If she could not love this man then she deserved to be beaten by some coal-heaver, and to scrub his floors. She had always lamented the fact that all men seemed to be brutally thoughtless flesh-seekers, or sensible, dreamless ciphers, or subtle but thin-skinned weaklings, and Chamberlain was none of the three. His mind held a charming deadlock between elderly and adolescent qualities, and his emotions could be plain and indirectly twink-ling by turns, and his body—was that the hindrance? Did she fail to love him because his nose was too large and his shoulders not broad enough, and be-cause he was a little bow-legged? Good God, had she been deceiving herself with wails about mental stimulation when all that she wanted was a well-shaped, youthful man who would agree with most of her opinions? If she couldn't love Chamberlain, she would prove that she had lied to herself for years.

"I don't know whether I love you, Bob, but I know that I ought to," she said. "You're the most intelligent and understanding man I've ever met, and I deserve to be thrashed for not throwing myself at you, but I want to be honest with you. I've been telling myself that I didn't love you because it didn't seem to matter whether you touched me or not, but that's not a final proof. I don't think people can really know whether they love each other until they've rested in each other's arms. Of course, if they're absolutely indifferent, or if they hate each other, then it's a simple thing, but otherwise they're only guessing, and wondering, and fearing. While you were gone, I made up my mind to ask you to take me, and I would have if you hadn't spoken first."

Her distressed frankness held him motionless for a time. It was hard to accept a woman whose uncertainty made the thing an announced experiment and not a joyous, unthinking contact. He wanted to hurt her and say inaudibly: "If you don't love me, then you'll have a remembrance that will always punish you just as I'm punishing you now," and hold her because it meant immediate pleasure while tomorrow might be void and lonely, but the other part feared that he might injure and disappoint both of them, and warned him to wait until she embraced him of her own accord. Puzzled by his stillness and silence, Jessica placed her arm around his shoulders and kissed his cheek. The touch of her killed all of his thoughts in a second's space. His mind changed to a fire that burned without glowing—a black heat —and his emotions were dervishes. He kissed her face, and throat, as though he were drinking from the curves of some transfigured fountain, and his hands sought her with the alternate fierceness and gentleness with which a lover abuses and doubts the precarious reality of his beloved one.

Jessica held a stubborn, dreading tenderness and said to herself again and again: "I want to love him,

I want to love him," as if the words could pound
her into a forgetful acceptance of their meaning.

*   *   *

The past night returned to her in each successive
detail. All that had happened was an aching tense-
ness, and a diffused relief, and a sense that something
had hovered over her and then avoided her. Her
contact with Chamberlain had subsided to the mild-
est of endearments on his part with poetic lines im-
provised to her eyes and breasts, while she had
grown tentatively motherly, to spare him the knowledge of her disappointment, and had tried to
imitate a grateful affection which was not within
her.

As she looked at Chamberlain now, she had an
impulse to depart without awakening him. Otherwise, there would be the usual aftermaths of such a
night—setting your shoulders to the weight of
reality, and caressing each other because both of you
wanted to act as though you were still unqualifiedly
precious to each other and not the least bit drained
and prosaic, and talking briskly to keep up the illusion of an undiminished charm. Even when people
loved each other, waking up together in the morning
must have something of a denuded ordeal about it.
Why didn't they slip away from each other in the
darkness and return on the next night, with all of
the mystery and freshness revived? Since she did

not love Chamberlain, she felt that it might be a calamity to stay with him and wait for him to wake up.

She pulled down a shade at one of the curtained windows, to keep the approaching sun from rousing him—it was barely dawn—and then she managed to leave without disturbing him, telling him in a note pinned to her pillow that she would see him on the following evening. She decided that most of her emotional failures might be due to the fact that she needed to be slowly awakened.

*   *   *

During the next seven days she visited Chamberlain's apartment every night. She told him in advance that she would always leave him immediately after he had fallen asleep, and when he asked her why she answered that it was dangerous and vitiating for a man and woman to stay with each other when the earth was heavily beckoning to their feet. He laughed and said that if two human beings couldn't peacefully retain their value to each other every morning then they were lower than animals in the fields, but she replied that on the contrary only the most sensitive men and women were averse to an over-familiar proximity after they had been with each other. It seemed a small matter to argue about, and he gave in without many words, but it left him mildly disquieted—it was so entirely un-

like the unreasoning, lingering thank-you of a woman
in love.   After the first night he did not ask her
again whether she loved him, taking it for granted
that she would not have become his mistress otherwise, and dimly squelching the fear that her answer
might be a negative one.   He half-sensed, at times,
the   dismay,   deliberation   and   self-goading   with
which she yielded to him, but he could not quite
admit that his perceptions were right, since it would
have crushed him, and he repeated to himself that
she was a woman who feared to give all of herself
lest it should spell the end of intimacy, and fought
against it, and reluctantly retreated.

The least plausible explanation is welcome to a
man who loves a woman, for unless she is obviously
prostrate, he teeters desperately on the brink of each
night and does not dare to question her own love,
since her answer might shove him into blackness.
To Jessica, her experiences with Chamberlain
grew different only in that she became more
practiced in her dissimulations and consoled herself
with the thought that she was making him happy
while the cost to her was but a few, endurable hours.
But such experiences remain desirable to a woman
only for a short time, and only because she dreads
the thought of slaying the man's delight, in a rudely
ungraceful way, and still preserves a mote of hope
that her emotions will increase for him.

At the end of the first week, after stealing from him at dawn, Jessica rested in her apartment and considered the situation. While she had hunted for a taxi-cab driver on the semi-deserted, quaintly ugly streets, several male stragglers had squinted at her, with an appraising, derogatory, and often carelessly ogling mien, as though to say: 'Hmm, well-dressed, shapely wench pushed out by her master, eh? Wouldn't he give you a roof till afternoon?" and one middle-aged reveler in evening clothes had muttered an obscene request and placed his fumbling hands upon her, forcing her to flee down the street. These incidents bloomed hugely in her fertile mood and gave her a common, prominently ticketed feeling. Her life was rendering her open to imputations and affronts which had no right to intrude upon her, and the men on the street had not been entirely wrong after all. She was nearing the condition of a prostitute by giving herself to a man whom she did not love, merely because she felt that she had abruptly hurt other men and wanted to make amends, and because the moderate pleasure which he gave her was better than a sexual void—or was it better?—and because she liked his mind and deemed it worthy of the favor of her body. An unconvincing array! A prostitute received money and squirmed through her business hours with an efficient boredom—at least it was probable that she did, although Jessica had never known one—and found at rare times some handsome, soft-voiced man with whom she could restore part of the vanished thrill, while she, Jessica, was virtually selling herself for nothing and counterfeiting emotions which the prostitute honestly denied (their "love yous" and "honeys" were understood to be false both by themselves and the men whom they were with) ! As for Chamberlain's happiness, she would probably lead it to an even more severe blow if she deferred from killing it now. He would become more and more dependent upon her and deluded, whereas, if she left him now, he would feel a great wrench but it would be one from which he might more easily recover. Besides, her hope of eventually abandoning herself to him was almost extinct, and it would be ridiculous to let him take what should have been the sincere boon of her body week after week on the slim chance that she might gradually become one with him.

He had been somewhat drunk on the preceding night—drunk enough to be more insistent than graceful—and she was strewn with bruises left by his hands—marks that should have been the cherished mementos of an equal wildness on her part, and not reminders of unwished-for pain ! She, Jessica Maringold, who could have herded ten men

together with each of her little fingers, was submitting to the maltreatment of one man whom she
did not love! The thing was becoming debasing.
But outside of her distraught egotism, a greater
lesson confronted her in this experience. She had
found out that she could not physically love men
who were intellectual, and considerate, and clear-
hearted—the one man who had come nearest to
arousing her sex was Purrel, a mental idiot, and a
ruffian beneath all of the false genialities given to
him by money and position. She would have to
choose between men who could bring her sexual
completion and leave her mind untouched and even
sneering, and men who could supply her with ideas,
and contradictions, and wit, without affecting her
tangible self. On one side there was mingled rhap-
sody and rest for the real nerves of her body, and
on the other side a morose, fluctuating, neurasthenic
shadow. . . . Since part of her dissatisfaction
would always remain, it was best to end the physical half of it. Mentally, she might reach a point
where she could delve solely into her own resources,
but physically this would be impossible.

She recalled her caresses with Purrel and how
they had concentrated and renewed her, as though
she had been on the rim of a blissfully frightened
dream and had not fallen into it because of her determination to remain balanced and resentful to a

man who did not deserve her. It had been the opposite with Chamberlain—a longing to fall into the dream and an inability to effect it. Undoubtedly, all that was left was a marriage to Purrel, or to some other man of his kind, and the continuation of her painting, now and then, to keep herself from feeling too creatively effaced, although she would be in reality.

She sat at her desk and wrote the following letter to Chamberlain:

"Bobsie Dear,

It's always useless to write to somebody that you're going to part from—meanly, dismally useless—and it even looks cowardly. As though you had to tell it from a distance. But if I sat beside you and told you, you'd beg me to stay, or I'd look at your face and then relent against my will, and that would be the worst thing that could happen to both of us. I can't give you the love that you need, and if I kept on trying to, I'd only hurt you so badly in the end that you might never care to hunt for it again. I haven't been dishonest with you—I told you from the beginning that it was an experiment on my part. If I knew why I didn't love you, then sex would be a magical slave just waiting for me to call him, and not what it is—a haughty, shrouded master who refuses to speak to me. I hope, Bobsie, that you won't hate me, unless it will comfort you any. I did want to make you happy, but I see now that I was only cruel to you and negligent to myself. . . . I won't end with any conventional 'I'll always remember you,' because that's such an easy, cheap thing to say, but you've filled my heart with newness and unrest, and if you ever do die out of my memory it will be very slowly. If we hadn't taken each other we might still come together, and talk, and laugh, without the other thing, but it wouldn't be possible for us to return to our old friendship now. It would be just like trying to speak with a mouth stuffed with ashes! I'll never meet a man more entitled to my love than you are, and moments of real self-hatred will come back to me when I think of how I couldn't love you. That will be my retribution. I'm weeping invisibly as I write this.

JESSICA."

After she had read the letter she wanted to tear it up, for it seemed a little theatrical, and jerky, and had a despairing sentimentality that did not sound real, whereas she had desired to write a clearly regretful, self-belittling letter, neither too intense nor too restrained. As she reflected, however, she concluded that if she wrote and tore up ten more letters none of them would be much of an improvement on this first one. Letters of farewell, in which one person was taking the initiative against the desire of the other, were at best over-stressed, guilty, uneven expressions, unless the writer was a literary creator, and even then the letter would probably be a deftly comfortless species of essay-writing. In your anxiety not to harm the other person any more than you had, your words merely dodged about, and their underlying sharpness refused to be slain. She sealed the letter and went to bed, for she had slept little during her past night.

When Chamberlain received the missive, he paced up and down in his apartment and assured himself that he was bitterly thunderstruck at her sudden withdrawal, but this stagy feeling—the shiver of his egotism as it kept its size from decreasing—did not remain long. He admitted to himself that he had expected this occurrence ever since his first night with her, and that he had filled himself with whisky on their last night to kill his presentiment that their parting was imminent. Did anything on earth ever last, and wasn't it always a matter of frightenedly grasping at happiness because you could spy its folded talons and reveled in the sensation of keeping them powerless for a while? Yet, a week was

such a flitting respite—if she had only stayed a
month, or two, he would have felt more substan-
tially rewarded, and then he might have relinquished
her with a complacent sneer at the thoroughness with
which he had drained her, instead of feeling that she
had grazed his limbs and vanished! The latter was
an unworthy thought, but, well, since when did lust
ever pretend to be kindly? Sooner or later it came
down to the question of which one would be the
first to harm the other, unless you took a woman
for a night, in which case your emotions were simply
marking time in a careless feast ended by the morning activities. Why had Jessica been unable to love
him? He discarded the explanations that would
have made him feel important, and settled it by telling himself that she had a streak of the courtesan
in her—perhaps more than a streak—and wanted
to be manhandled, and indifferently treated, and
subtly derided, whereas he had courted her at
length, and had feared to give her physical pain,
and had been close to juvenile in his delicate requests
and considerations. It would have been better if
he had spiritually struggled with her on the first
night of their meeting and then walked away with
the airiest of cynicisms—in that case their positions would have been reversed and she would have
pursued him with the most piqued of longings. The
next time he met an intelligent woman, whose face
and body were as ravishing as her mind, he would

make love to her first and resume the conversation afterwards. If he had to lose her, it might as well happen in one night as in seven. He resolved not to answer Jessica's letter, and to make no efforts to see her—if there was a remote chance of her coming back to him, it would only thrive upon his silence and absence.

*   *   *

On the following day, Jessica purchased her passage for New York, but the sailing date was two weeks away, and she decided to shun the "1919 Club" and the studios which she had frequented, for fear of running into Chamberlain, and do nothing but paint and read. Such accidental meetings were always gruesome, with their unavailing words or sorry, hostile silences. On the third day before her departure, as she was walking down Haymarket Street after having cashed a check at the American Express Company office, she was stopped by Joseph Israel. They chatted in an amiable, careful manner, and then he urged her to dine with him. She hesitated, for she was enjoying the feeling of being an unsexed, unsought creature, but she decided that a few hours with him would loosen her mind and give her thoughts a chance to play a bit. After the dinner he proposed a theater, but she declined and said that drama on the stage was always unconvincing unless you were in a credulous, nervous mood, whereupon he invited her to continue the conversation in his apartment, and she accepted.

Would he begin to make love to her?—she shrugged her shoulders. A last, fleeting escapade, before she returned to America and marriage, would be a fitting joke on her previous hopes and writhings, and at any rate the whole question was too exquisitely trivial to consider. She liked Israel's heavy, bantering jeers at life and its people, broken at times by an unwilling sentimentality which he stifled immediately after its utterance—all Jews of any culture and intelligence seemed to have this shamefaced shifting between cynicism and an underlying softness, and Israel was a sublimated Levine in that respect—but he had no power to affect her emotions as far as she could see. His slight figure, and the hump in his nose, and his over-wide lips made her regard him, physically, as an approach to Caliban.

They sipped Chartreuse and Burgundy in his apartment and spoke about the freaks and dotards in Literary London. The liqueurs made her light-headed and indifferent, and she began to wish that he would drop his false face and woo her—nothing in the world mattered, and it would be pleasant to remind him teasingly of that fact as he fervently sought her. He asked her to sit upon the couch beside him and look at an etching which he had bought on the previous day—the light was better there. After she had complied and they had scanned the etching for a moment, he turned and commenced to embrace her, without as much as a preliminary kiss, and without uttering a word, as though it were a pressing and understood matter that needed no hedging, or gilding. She resisted him angrily for a time—was he out of his head, and did he think that she was a supine trollop, who would yield to the most instant and careless advances from any man? —but against her will she found herself slipping into a mood of hilarious relief. This was an even better repetition of her night with Levine—an affair without long-worded, candid explanations, and tentative contacts, and assertions of unusual affection. It dismissed all of the perturbations and coquetries of sex, and was the viciously simple confession of a man that he desired a woman for no other reason than that they happened to be alone together and she was physically attractive. It was crude, and real, and made the rest of love seem to be a hectic, fanciful bleating and retreating over nothing in particular.

Afterwards, he offered her another glass of Chartreuse and went on talking as though nothing had happened, and she fell into his spirit and wondered why she had ever looked upon sex as an elusive burden. For the first time she had fully given herself to a man, with all of her restraints and deliberations changed to a soaring oblivion—a man whom she did not love in the least and might never meet again: a man who was almost physically repulsive to her. She was still smiling, in spite of the headache brought by the wines, as she rode back to her apartment.

PART THREE

PART THREE

JESSICA reclined in one of the bedrooms of her house on Riverside Drive, New York, and read the book of verse which a young poet had thrust upon her at the end of the previous night. She had met him at one of those ribald, gross, not quite frenzied, sexually maladroit costume balls staged by artists every autumn and winter in the uptown New York hotels, with the connivance of smart and jaded society people—a chance to be devilish, and frothily dictating, and scantily clad— if you were a woman—until tomorrow called you a liar and brought back the tame and fully dressed epilogue. The young poet had competed with other men for her dances and had won most of them because he talked nonsense that was not quite stupid, and had eyes that begged without losing their self-control, and fox-trotted with a delirious strut that just missed being obscene, whereas the dancing of the other men was either epicine or inept. At a ball, you wanted a man to be sportive, and even gayly imbecilic, and yet have him convey the impression that he was a hundred times more intelligent and had merely thrust aside his real self for the night. Otherwise what choice was left? Clowns, roughneck Don Juans, urbane fakers, fishy-eyed business men, imperturbable, solid-looking youths—you took them in rotation because they were something for your sex to lean upon and move with in the dances.

Jessica had worn a street-urchin's costume, with bare legs, short, ragged trousers, and a man's soft-collared, gray shirt open at the throat, and the young poet had judged her to be an artist's model, or a chorus girl more wistful and refined than her kind. He was a tall youth who wore his dress-suit as though he wished it were absent, and he had a humorous, bluntly molded, ruddy face. At the end of the ball he had asked Jessica if he could accompany her to her home, and after she had assented, he had been overawed at the sight of her limousine and uniformed chauffeur. Who was she —the mistress of a wealthy man, or some society woman? In the first case he would have to "go slow" but in the second he might find a patroness for his work.

During the ride to her home he commenced to fondle Jessica and her acquiescence induced him to start a more impetuous approach, whereupon she pushed him away and laughed.

"Silly kid, don't you know that an automobile's impossible," she said. "Besides, you mustn't work so fast. No man's really subtle, but some men can make you believe they are, and that's the kind that women fall for."

"Thanks for the instructions, but I'll probably

disregard them," he answered. "If sex mattered much to me I'd think about the moves, like a game of chess, but it doesn't. It's just a physiological interval between the words I put on paper. If you didn't take it sometimes you'd become too much aware of your body, and that would interfere with the things you write. Frankly, if you were another good-looking woman I'd hug you just the same."

"What a hopelessly normal attitude," said Jessica. "Of course, you don't begin to live up to it but you like to hear yourself say it anyway. I know a line from a book that fits you perfectly."

"What is it—I'll bite," he answered.

" 'Sen-ti-men-tal-i-ty boldly whistling to keep up its courage.' After I've been drinking all night I always say something difficult like that, an' if I can pronounce it clearly then I know I'm not drunk."

"Well, mine's been whistling so long that it's permanently forgotten itself," he replied.

When they stood in the entrance of her house, he asked if he could come in.

"Dear boy, you probably don't know that I'm a married woman," said Jessica. "My husband's gone to Boston for two days, but it's barely possible that he might come back on the 4 A.M. train this morning, and melodrama's getting commonplace nowadays."

"I'm sorry that you're so fond of living," he answered. "There isn't much of a lure to life, you know, except when we lie about it and tell ourselves how reckless and unique we are. We're not, really, but we need a bold fraud now and then—it keeps the next morning from being too insipid and too cautious."

"I'd never have guessed it if you hadn't told me," said Jessica. "Your lecture is out of place. I've been ever so reckless for years, and I didn't need to lie about it either."

This didactic, sanguine youth, with his fresh, half-homely face, reminded her of a lost babe striving to be at ease—they always pretended to be very experienced and weary because they were afraid that you would refuse them if they acted eager. Yet this was their main appeal—it was hard to reject the beseeching, piteous, little masquerade.

"You can come in for a while but you've got to be very quiet," she said. "I've seven servants sleeping on the top floor and they're apt to come down if they hear any suspicious noises."

Jessica sat with him on a broad divan in the front parlor. She was still in her street-urchin's costume and looked as though she had mistakenly wandered into the broad, high-ceilinged, ornate room.

"I've given you a wrong opinion of me," he blurted out at last. "You think I'm just a sensual kid, I know, but I can be quite ascetic at times. I don't just want to have you now and never see you again. I'd like to be friends with you, too."

"Don't spoil it all," answered Jessica. "Be sophisticated to the bitter end."

Nettled by her raillery, he became furiously demonstrative, and she accepted his embraces in a spirit of reproving laughter. Sex had ceased to mean more to her than a nervous satisfaction stripped of all glosses and curiosities. Have it over with, if the man refreshed and melted you now and then, and think of something else until the next episode.

Before leaving her, he took a volume of his verses from a leather case and gave it to her.

"After you read these poems you'll want to see me again," he said, "because they're full of everything I wanted to say to you, and didn't. I don't suppose any poet ever talks half as well as he writes. When he's talking to another person words seem to be overworked and hopeless to him and he almost hates to use them."

"I didn't ask you to give me an essay, you foolish boy," answered Jessica, moved by a whim to soothe his egotistic distress.

Now, as she rested in her bedroom, almost twenty-four hours later, she threw the book aside and yawned. Broken up, and sometimes subtle verse, of a light caliber, very mischievous in its disregard of punctuation and grammar, and all to distract your attention from its basic sentimentality. She forgot the book and its author without the least effort— he was merely one of six men with whom she had

had one-night affairs during the past year, and the number had not been larger because she insisted upon selecting men with some semblance of brains, and passable faces, and youth, and because she had not yet reached the point where she wanted sexual indulgence to become a nondescript routine.

Her mood was lazy and unexpectant, and she fell into a revery in which past incidents came and disappeared in a detached fashion. Over three years had elapsed since her return from London, and they had wrought several changes within her. She was more composed and jovially inconsiderate in her treatment of people—a cool and at times even tart selfishness that said: "Take it or leave it—I don't care much"—and she gave herself to unimpeded pleasures and driftings, with no great concern. Most of her dreams about "self-expression" and "mental comradeship" had died, but she mocked herself by feebly reviving the scant remainder now and then. Life became slower and less startling every year, even though the change was not perceptible enough to make you completely downcast, and you had to make some pretense of spurring on its heart and soul, no matter how forlorn and irregular your attempts were. She still painted in a desultory manner, and wrote her day's happenings in a diary and grinned sorrowfully at them (a covert unbending to sentiments that were not quite dead).

Purrel had courted her again, upon her return from London, and had manifested a chastened and unprotesting spirit. Yes, he knew that he was a quick-tempered brute at times, and was too prone to measure everything with the length of a dollar bill, but he asserted that he wanted her to help him in overcoming these traits and looked up to her as the only person who could alter him to any great extent. His motives were mixed ones. He felt that he could win her back only through a huge amount of careful dissembling, but he was also more aware of her mental domination and more inclined to listen to it. There was no holding out against the fact that she had a wonderful mind, even if it was misdirected, and she could probably have gone into his own office and made twice as much money as he did, if she had wanted to. If he could marry her, he would have the feeling of owning a woman who was his superior and reducing her to a seeming equality with him—excellent, if she could be induced not to "rub it in." During her absence he had trotted around with several girls and had missed the aching tumult and joyous after-dazes which Jessica alone had given him. He had no other way of explaining it except to contend that Jessica and he were natural mates in spite of their different ideas and habits. The exact features, and figure, and voice of one woman hit you in just the right spot and appealed to you much more than those of any other woman because you had been made to fit into one kind only. You might not be forever faithful to her after marrying her but she would always remain the one woman who had completely satisfied your sex and fondled your emotions. That was the only reason for marriage—outside of your desiring a son to live after you—for otherwise you didn't care to be with any woman for more than a restricted length of time.

Jessica had finally agreed to marry Purrel because he had become much less aggressive and blatant, and because she had determined to narrow most of her life to sexual pleasures, and unhurried enjoyments and escapades in between, and he met the first requirement better than any other man whom she knew, and life had taught her not to gamble too much where sex was concerned. Now that he seemed to be tamed and a little self-inspecting, it might be possible to live with him without any senseless frictions and to ignore him when he was not caressing her. Of course, she would have to keep up some show of respecting his affairs and ideas, but that would not be an over-arduous deceit. Her father had gleefully received the news of her engagement to Purrel and had insisted upon making them a present of the house in which they were now living, while her Aunt Roberta had felicitated her on not having fallen in love with some eloquent wastrel or poverty-stricken youth. Their attitudes had meant little to Jessica—it was pleasant that they were happy about it, but if they had been unhappy she would not have allowed them to deter her. Old people, especially those nearest to

you, were always intent upon having you do something that would tell them that their own lives had
been discerning and justified—an incentive to fight
back, if it intruded upon you, and the wanest of
jests if it failed to bother you. She was melted a
bit by her father's garrulous raptures, but this was
no more than the indolent zest which she derived
from satisfying another person, to whom she was
indebted, at no cost to her emotions.

She passed through the solemn flourishes of a wed-
ding in one of the largest Episcopalian churches in
the city, with hundreds of society people in the
pews, and felt that there was something indecent
about formally and publicly proving that you were
going to sleep with one man for the remainder of
your nights—a misleading proof in the bargain—
but this provoked nothing more than a smile within
her. Poor people, how they would have yielded to
consternation if she had cried out in the midst of
the ceremony: "Come on, let's put a little pep
in this thing! You always make a marriage look
and sound like a cross between a bedroom announce-
ment and a mournful contradiction. Let's have some
jazz music and laugh it off!" No matter how tat-
tered the veils were, they had to serve because no
one was courageous enough to invent anything to
take their place.

Purrel, on the other hand, had felt tenderly erect
and almost shining with importance—a beautiful girl

was confiding herself to his appreciation and care, and a newer and more responsible life had begun.

They went to Paris, during the week after their marriage, and loitered there for a month. Purrel abstained from drinking too much, and was taciturn and even deferential at times, and Jessica gave herself to sex and minor recreations with the blankest of heads and a feeling of giddy supremacy. This was life—the warm, shallow, lightly disturbing thing that slipped away almost before you knew that it was with you, and made you seize the surfaces of it with a hasty despair.

When they returned to New York she kept up her hoydenish, never-still existence for a year, and remained faithful to Purrel—embraces with men in the hilarity of ballrooms and parties didn't count—and congratulated herself on the fact that he had become a remarkably quiet, considerate nonentity, while Purrel was generous to her whims and surrendered himself to a life that had become even more dominantly sexual than usual, with his nights separated by financial pursuits. At the end of their first year of marriage, however, the situation between them began to change. Grudgingly but surely, Purrel was forced to admit that his sexual desires for Jessica were not as strong as they had been— the imploring, over-awed possession of one who remained piquantly strange even in the midst of close contacts, and the lengthy deliriums, had vanished. She was now a pretty, shapely, well-absorbed woman, who gave him the same clear and moderate enjoyment which he had experienced from other women before his marriage. He looked forward to his nights with her with a snug, approving feeling, but with no impatient anticipations. Other women whom he met here and there restored his curiosity, and he began to reflect on the possibility and difference of possessing them, and the refreshing novelties that he was missing.

He told himself that marriage was always like this—the first, inexplicable "kick" couldn't stay forever, and you and your wife had to settle down to a steadier and milder pace—and that it was his duty to remain faithful to Jessica because she was a "high-class," still beautiful woman who trusted him. These reasons, however, did not seem to be very potent to him when he stood or sat beside a particularly handsome or plumply angelic-faced woman, who showed him that she would not have been averse to his solicitations. Hell, life was a short proposition, and you were a fool if you turned your back upon every exceptional chance for enjoyment. Besides, he wanted to feel that he was a conquering, sought-after man again, who could pick and choose among women—when you everlastingly chained yourself to one woman you became little more than her trousered servant, and you grew virtually effeminate in the process. The sanctity of your marriage vows?—rats. No one really believed in them and very few people carried them out, and when they did they were usually compelled to for some reason outside of their desire. Take the Farringtons, for instance—she was homely and unaccomplished and he weighed close to two hundred and twenty and had an enormous double chin and knew that no woman could possibly fall in love with him except for his money. Again, there were other couples who were simply afraid of inviting comments and "slams"—funny mice who hugged some one else in the gayety of a party, or in the shadows at a garden affair, and then scampered back to their husbands or wives. Most of the men under middle age whom Purrel knew were not faithful to their wives after the second or third year of marriage, but their digressions were irregular and well covered. They had no definite mistresses who might "raise a row" and break up the man's home life, but they picked out women whom they would never see again, or women who could be merrily casual about such matters, or women of the theater who changed their "papas" at least once a month.

Purrel realized that it would not be easy to hoodwink a woman of Jessica's canny and alert kind, and that it would be too risky to take any of the women in his own and Jessica's social gang, or to cavort with women who lived in New York. He began to take "business trips" to Boston, of two or three days' duration, and to revel there with chorus girls and street "pick-ups." . . . Jessica immediately sensed his infidelity—his returns, with

flowers, candy, bloodshot eyes, and nervously re-
doubled caresses were so transparent—and the
knowledge made her slightly annoyed, and meditative. Well, her sexual convenience had grown tired
of her, while she—how did she feel? Sex had become a matter-of-fact, well-plumbed, softly agreeable thing to her, and she had been faithful to her
husband because she had been convinced that he
was as sexually satisfying as any other man would
be, but now that he had been audacious enough to
show her the way, there were equally alluring men
with fresher tactics, who would plead with her and
restore her feeling of coquettish sovereignty. Besides, it would be heartening once more to have
experiences with men who could utter clever sentences and incite your conjectures as to what they
would say next—Purrel was growing more stupid
and fixed every day. A man's mind wasn't indispensable to sexual enjoyment—she had found that
out long ago—but still it could embellish your contacts with him, especially after you had been deprived of it for over a year and a half. Again,
Purrel must be deriving a sweet feeling from knowing that she was reserved for him alone while he
philandered wherever he pleased. She would take
away his conspiring conceitedness, and if he raved
over the fact that she was emulating him, the divorce courts were always open.

When he departed for Chicago, to supervise a
bond transaction, she drove down to a tea room in

the "bohemian" section and coolly selected the most handsome and sprightly tongued, unattended man in the place, and spent the night at his studio, and felt hilariously relieved afterwards. He had been a slender, Italian youth, with a loosely dissipated, long-nosed face, and graceful manners, and he confided to her the story of his past—how he had been an officer in the Italian navy and had been charged with the embezzlement of his ship's fund and forced to flee to America until the matter "blew over" and he could return to Italy. Jessica had feigned an overwhelming interest in the tale—it never mattered whether their stories were true or untrue, for life was little more than a night's boasting until the interference of daylight—and she had cuddled in his arms and delighted herself by playing the part of the credulous baby deceived by the worldly sinner. He had guessed her to be an unusually naïve woman stealing a night away from her husband, and he had vainly sought to learn her address or telephone number before they parted, but she had evaded his efforts and promised to call on him "some afternoon."

After Purrel returned from Chicago they had their first, open quarrel. Ever since their marriage he had wanted her to bear him a child, and she had refused with the flippant statement that she had no intention of losing her figure for at least three or four years, while he had yielded because he had been too much under her physical spell to wrangle with her. Now, he continued to importune her, and when she still refused he called her unnatural and trivially selfish, and said that she cared only to romp about and had no realization of the duties and serious tasks in life. When she replied that his definition of the duties in life consisted of innumerable "business trips," with women and liquor as an accompaniment, and that he would have to excuse her if her own definition were equally elastic, he became guiltily enraged and longed to strike her, and barely held himself back because he was afraid that such an act might cause her to leave him. For the first time, he doubted her faithfulness to him and lost his feeling of complacent, half-repentant treachery, and felt instead outwitted and insecure. A wife had no right to follow her husband's freedom—somehow, when a woman gave herself to men she ruined her value and spoiled her distinctively secretive body, whereas a man could offer himself to many women and still remain the same because he was sturdier, and less easily marked and crushed. Again, men were really receivers and gave little of themselves to any woman, while the yielding of women was much more complete and intense.

He asked Jessica outright whether she had taken any other man since their marriage and she answered impudently that he would have to find that out for himself. Since he had no evidence against her and she had not confessed, he clung to the saving idea that she had merely taunted him on her own side because she suspected his transgressions. It would be useless to watch her closely because she had but to wait until his next journey if she wanted to be intimate with another man— unless you were innocent yourself you made a poor detective. Well, there was nothing that he could do until he caught her with a man, in open dallying, and then he would beat up the man, give her a share of the blows, and divorce her. But even if his suspicions were unfounded, she would have to "come down from her high horse"—she was becoming too nastily independent and derogatory to him, and no spirited man could live with a woman who refused to be his subordinate in any matter —it broke the backbone of the traditional supremacy to which men were entitled as the stronger, bread-winning sex.

Then Jessica's father died, in an automobile accident, and the happening gave her a sober, self-reproaching feeling that was not grief, but verged upon it because she longed to be sorrowful and felt that it would be inhuman if she were otherwise. This limited, jovial, material man had once held her child-form in his arms and crooned over it, and had fought to protect her helplessness, and had loved her in his own near-sighted, guilty, and partly selfish way—you couldn't brush aside such things, regardless of the fact that you and your father had never had any real communion. They persisted, and left reminiscent quivers in your heart, and made you feel ashamed because you were not shattered and anguished at his death. She was even able to weep at her father's funeral—tears that were more self-rebuking than genuine—and she went into a comparative seclusion for the following year, and abandoned her parties and dances, and went back to her painting and the reading of books.

Purrel felt that she was deeply grief-stricken and that he must respect her feelings and leave her alone as much as possible—there is something softly wary in the way in which even the coarsest of men greet the phenomenon of death—while she took advantage of his delusion and avoided him most of the time. Their sexual contacts became more and more occasional, and he fell into the habit of visiting the apartments of certain actresses whom he had known in the past, and returning home at 1 A.M., so that he would not incriminate himself and could assert that he had spent an evening at his club, if she questioned him. Toward the end of the year, however, the dissensions between himself and Jessica reappeared. He opened up the old question of her becoming a mother and she replied that she was not certain whether she wanted him to be the father of any children that she might have, which angered him so much that he seized several plates from the breakfast-table and threw them to the floor, and rushed out of the room. He still did not quite dare to hit her—held back by his old

fear of her gigantic pride—and the inanimate objects had been the only things against which he
could vent his feelings. Outside of his desire for
a son, he felt that the situation was growing impossible in other ways. The will of Jessica's father
had left her the bulk of his estate, after comfort-
ably providing for her aunt, Roberta, and leaving
small sums to other relatives, and she now had
four million dollars in real estate, bonds, and cash.
How was it possible to issue commands to a woman
who was four times wealthier than he was and could
quit him at any time with a feeling of insolent
security? If a wife was not materially dependent
upon her husband, he lost one of the most reliable
methods of cowing her, and no other way remained,
except physical punishment. It depressed a man
to feel that his wife was both mentally and finan-
cially superior to him, and the infinite masculine
swagger and authority essential to his being had to
flee to other women, who would babble with delight
if he gave them a check or bought them a diamond-
studded bracelet.

He decided to make his infidelity so apparent
that she would be induced to divorce him—his maltreated pride told him that he should not even
deign to discuss the matter with her—and he began
to stay away from their residence for entire nights,
but when she met him on the following night she
always laughed and made some remark to the effect
that she hoped that his previous evening had been

as amorously successful as her own. Scowling and oppressed, he would walk off and wonder how he could extricate himself from a situation that had grown unendurable. When people of absolutely alien temperaments marry each other, for purely physical reasons, the end is always that the weakest one becomes filled with a profitless hatred, while the strongest one grows amiably indifferent. With the lowering of the physical attraction that brought them together, the least thoughtful of the two desires to replace it with an arbitrary meanness— "Even if we no longer love each other, you'll do what I tell you to do!"—while the other cares only to withdraw with the smallest amount of friction and recrimination.

To Jessica, Purrel had become a dolorous, immovable, protesting joke—a man who wanted to be respectable, and a roaming pagan, at the same time, and was angry because she would not lend herself to this duality and wait at home, with folded hands, until her lord was ready to leave his mistresses and bring her the blessings of motherhood (most men were excruciatingly comical). She felt that there would be no need to divorce him until she met a man with whom she wanted to have at least one child, in which case it would be necessary to divorce Purrel and marry the other man, to give her offspring a name.

Now, as she rested within her bedroom, she was in a plaintive, speculative, enervated mood—sex, money, merriment, what did they all amount to except a few triumphant falsehoods that grew much less triumphant with every year, a few headaches and early-morning inertias, a few snatchings at stars that turned out to be cloth ones sewed to the blue top of a circus tent, and a few, unexpected visitations of pain just when you felt that you would never experience them again. Perhaps she ought to be of some good in the world, and devote most of her fortune to combating disease and ignorance among human beings—she smiled wanly at the suggestion. Curious, wasn't it, that such great, charitable impulses always came when you were most dangerously aware of your insignificance and so inclined to turn to your money, as a chance for kindly despotism which you were neglecting. The use of billions of dollars could never wipe out the superstitions and fears of human beings, and all of the sanitary, and scientific, and educational devices and researches of her time were doomed to be destroyed and forgotten by the struggling cruelty of men bent upon slaying each other—the idea wasn't her own (she had read it in a recent book), but it was certainly a true prophecy. No, she would continue to help out artists and writers, who had something unconsciously defiant within them that too many people didn't care to see or hear—just for the perversity of avenging a similar self within her that had never unfolded—and continue to send her checks to relief drives for children and poverty-stricken mothers, and let it go at that.

One of the doors to the large bedroom opened and Purrel walked in, stepping gingerly and striving not to sway too much, as a man does when he has imbibed a great deal of liquor but is still proudly convinced of his sobriety. He had come from a suburban roadhouse, where he had quarreled with his inamorata of the night and left her in hysterics and in his head was a hazy, vicious resolve to "have it out" with Jessica and either beat her into a fearful respect or arrange for a permanent separation. When Jessica saw him she was surprised, since it was not his recent habit to enter her bedroom late at night. If his intentions were amorous, she would soon chase him out of the room—possibly his female of the night had disappointed him and he had been seized by a desire to turn to his wife for concrete consolation (what a pretty idea). If he had only intruded for the purpose of quarreling about the old —children—proposition, she would simply refuse to answer him and get rid of him as quickly and peacefully as she could.

He stood at the foot of the canopied, four-posted, walnut bed and glowered down at her. An excited jumble of words was in his head but each of them refused to give way to the other, and it was hard to shape his anger into speech. He wanted to rend her apart, with superbly scornful sentences, but the only expressions that occurred to him were out-bursts of profanity (you could frighten other women by cursing them, but Jessica wasn't built that way). She was clad in a peignoir of bluish gray silk, and in her shiftings on the bed it had become disar-ranged and partly exposed her body. As Purrel looked down at her, a desire to possess her rose within him, in spite of his anger, for his episode with the other woman in the roadhouse had not termi-nated to his best interests. Then his anger itself suggested that physical mastery would enable him to hurt her by mauling her flesh, under the pretext of rough fondness, and would also satisfy his sensual cravings, thwarted at the beginning of the night. She was too damn selfish to be affected by words, and only real pain could pierce her nature.

He sat on the edge of the bed and began to un-dress himself.

"We-e-ell, she wouldn't take Teddie to-night so he just had to come back to his neglected wife," said Jessica, in a voice of placid derision. "Isn't that too bad? But after all it isn't imperative—you can always telephone some other girl, you know. Go away, Teddie, please. I haven't the least desire to be with you."

"S'allright, you'll like me after I'm here a while," he answered. "I don't care 'bout other women—you're still there with me."

She could go on flinging her puny words—the

final remark would be his. Jessica rose from the bed and put on her slippers.

"Since you simply won't leave, you'll have to stay here alone," she said. "I'm going to sleep upstairs."

It was the best way to avoid an hour of wrangling and attempted caresses. She walked toward one of the doors and he darted after her, with the unsteady agility that semi-drunken men sometimes have, clutching one of her arms and swinging her around.

"What do you take me for—a damn fool?" he asked. "You've been lording it over me for months and I've got enough of it. I'd never have gone about with other women if you'd been willing to be a wife, and a mother, and not a common flirt with every man you happen to see. We weren't married two months before I saw Fred Rogers kissing you at a garden party. I let you get away with it because I thought you'd calm down and get responsible after a while, but I might have known different. You're just a damn, selfish, stuck-up woman, and all you can do is gab about a-art and let a gang of fourflushers milk you for all you're worth. You've got too much money for your own good—that's the trouble with you."

Jessica listened to his accusations and sneers with an unmoved weariness—what a mistake she had made in marrying this obtuse, obstreperous, singularly coarse man, whose only recourse was to defend his own jealous emptiness by throwing self-forgetful invectives at her.

"I don't care to join your sport of calling names," she replied, "and you're hardly qualified to give me any discourses on virtue. I was faithful to you until you began to sneak back from your wonderful trips to Boston, and then I remembered that there were other men not quite as boring as you are. . . . I suppose we'd better agree to leave each other, but we'll talk that over to-morrow, when you're sober —not now."

Her cool, distant words infuriated him, because she made his emotions cringe and falter in the midst of their denunciations, and because they could not bear the thought that she was realizing their discomfiture.

"I'm going to bo-ore you for one more night, anyway," he said, "and you'd better not try to leave this room, that's all."

He placed his arms around her waist and strove to drag her forward. She resisted him, and in their struggling her sleeveless peignoir slipped off. The sight and touch of her body—the only part of her that he had ever been able to reach—aroused a long-repressed devil within Purrel, and he began to beat her with his fists. The pain and effrontery of his blows made Jessica furious and she struck back at him and scratched his flesh in the effort to free herself, but she was not a match for his greater strength, and she became unconscious and sank to the floor.

When her senses returned, she found that she was resting upon the bed in the darkened room, and that Purrel had gone. She turned on the lights and stood unsteadily in front of a mirror, where she could see that one of her eyes was discolored, and her lips puffed out and clotted with blood, and her cheeks swollen, and her throat and breasts dotted with bruises. As she stood there, an unbelieving amazement transfigured her—Purrel had actually dared to beat her into insensibility and then . . . her hands doubled to fists and she stepped forward in the hot desire to pursue him and avenge herself, but she halted, appalled at the hopelessness of any physical retaliation. This was the century-old curse of her sex—a physical weakness that made a woman unprotected whenever a man chose to abandon his words and become brutally unscrupulous. She had read newspaper accounts of assaults on women and they had seemed to be such far-fetched, garbled melodramas—the man wasn't half to blame in most cases—but now she felt that she had joined a shame-faced band of women coarsely defiled against their will. In her over-wrought emotions, men took on a monstrous, hateful quality. Oh, she could kill Purrel for having dared to strike her and grasp her because the feebleness of his words and mind had been unable to cope with hers! What a contemptible, petty, frantic animal he was!

She did not want to call her maid because the maid might guess the cause of her mistress's condition, so she went to the medicine chest in another room and treated her bruises and returned to bed. As she tossed upon the bed—kept awake by the pain in her face and body—she laughed suddenly and inaudibly at the exaggeration and distress of her emotions. Purrel had temporarily marred her flesh because his egotism had become crazed by the knowledge that he could not mark and overcome her in any other way, but why was it more important than the attack of a pet dog would have been—a regrettable incident, but one that was inevitable when you allowed an utter animal to come close to you and then rejected its pawing? Her pride objected to her anger against Purrel, and she repeated to herself that she was conferring an over-dramatic honor upon the frenzy of a muscular pygmy, and that her emotions should subside to a practical, disgusted determination to divorce him and shun him for the rest of her life. She was not blameless herself, for she had continued to live with him and exasperate him with her flippant disparagements when it would have been wiser to remove herself from his frustrated desires.

He tried to see her on the following afternoon, but she refused to admit him into her room—the doors were locked—and sent him a message in which she informed him that she intended to procure a divorce. After his first feeling of discredited resentment—if there was any divorcing to be done, he'd be the one to do it—he became by degrees boisterously relieved. Thank God, the whole mess would soon be over, and then he would be able to marry some sensible, obedient, freshly girlish woman who would look up to him and appreciate his sturdy virtues, or else he could consort with admiring mistresses twice as good-looking and equally as brainy as Jessica was. His marriage to Jessica had taught him a great lesson—a man should never marry a woman unless she showed him that she was willing to bend to his authority, and unless she respected his position in the world. His physical desires for his wife never remained strong beyond a certain length of time, and when they began to decrease, he needed the compensation of being the untroubled, undisputed master of his home and his personal life. As for the woman, she still retained her beautiful clothes, and luxuries, and pleasures, and could still harmlessly flirt with other men, as long as she kept them from going too far, and had the additional satisfaction of raising a family of children and basking in their affection. Jessica was a freakish, posing, irresponsible, inordinately selfish woman, who was little better than a prostitute in her actions toward men, and whose endlessly mouthed reverence for a-art was merely voiced to keep people from seeing her emptiness. What had she ever done with that precious painting of hers—who was talking about it or praising it? He had known these things before he had married her, but he had allowed his intense, physical longing for her to lead him astray. Well, at any rate, he had given her something that she would never forget—the impact of his fists upon her face and body—and he had taught her that she could not lavish cheap, unmerited sarcasms and indignities upon a husband and escape from a deserved punishment!

Jessica remained in her room for several days, until her bruises had healed, and then she arranged a meeting with Purrel in the office of her lawyer, where the details of the divorce proceedings were agreed upon. Divorces are never difficult achievements when the interested parties are wealthy, and when they are both intent upon the same end, and when the situation is not complicated by questions of alimony and the custody of children. At the end of three months Jessica's marriage was canceled, and she celebrated the event by becoming dreamily and childishly drunk in a cabaret, and waking up the next morning to find herself ensconced in the apartment of a young actor, who had emerged victoriously from a fist-fight with her other suitors of the past night. The actor, a dark, robust man, with the seamed and broad-featured face of a prize-fighter, spoke as though it were taken for granted that she would remain with him—wealth and good looks, what luck!—but she treated him with a merry coolness that said: "It was true last night, and it's a lie now—like all other things—so let's forget about it!" She left him immediately and never saw him again, except from a distance. Even the best of men were usually charming and unsolved for only one night. On the second night they peeled off more than their visible garments and became just a bit stale and obvious. On the third night— but that was too shuddering to contemplate.

Jessica sold her house on Riverside Drive and went to live in a large suite of rooms in the most fashionable hotel in the city. Life to her had become nothing more than hosts of scampering nerve rituals, where laughter, disdain, impudence, vanity, and coquetry accepted one person and fled from another without desiring anything more than a perpetual shifting of episodes. She was not a creator, in spite of her clever stand-still with brushes and paint, and the idea of being a housewife was drolly repugnant, and the dismal, half-reckless, self-intrenched snobbishness of society life had been exhausted long ago, so what was left?—a hurried search for sensual and sensory incidents, and then the dark payment of middle age.

She drifted into the company of Broadway theatrical people and severed all of her connections with the society men and women with whom she had formerly mingled, and they were not loath to let her depart. In their estimation she was an over-risque, scatter-brained, insulting creature—it was all right to be somewhat risque, if you knew how to preserve a balance between your pranks and your responsibilities, but Jessica Maringold really carried it to a scandalous extreme and had ruined Bob Purrel's life, with her undiscriminating antics. Most of the actors and actresses with whom she mixed had a patented system for dealing with the wealthy women who figured in their night life—they uttered slangy, almost derogatory remarks to these feminine outsiders, with a laugh to take the sting away, and were careful to end up with compliments and the inference: "It was all in fun, old dear." This applied to the smaller fry, of course, for the top celebrities were either pompous, or blatantly unconcerned. Jessica knew that these people had no actual affection for her, and that they regarded her as "a sucker" or an appreciative after-theater audience, but she liked their persistent, strident artificialities. They were so accustomed to laughing, and weeping, and shifting in their rôles while on the stage, that they transported these characteristics to their off-stage hours and reiterated them until they changed from a conscious pose to a natural fickleness. Their craving for an audience made them alter all of life to a potential audience, and when they were in any gathering of human beings they were still "registering" and "putting it over," while even their most personal and private relations with men and women were never free from a tinge of hysterical posturing at best. It was the penalty which they paid for adapting themselves to the thoughts and emotions which other people ordered them to express behind the footlights, and to the tens of rôles which were often not a part of the actor's deeper nature, for thus they became eager to devise equally volatile and attractive lines and actions, when the grease paint was removed.

For the next two years, Jessica ran about with one theatrical crowd after another, and had brief affairs with some of the men, and entertained parties at her country home during the summer months, but toward the close of the second winter an incident occurred which gave her a stunned and sober mood.

She had been romping about with a picturesque, burly, hard-faced rake named Frederick Sariman, who was the comedian-star of popular musical comedies—a man with wasted eyes and a twitching mouth, who initiated her into the pleasures of heroin. She didn't care much for the heroin—it gave her a drowsy, lugubrious feeling and she envied the people who could take it and commence to pick rubies and sapphires from your clothes and hair—but she liked Sariman because he was the only absolutely reckless man that she had ever met. Life was a chance to curse, and fight, and swagger, to him, and thought was little more than a mumbled accompaniment to these major ends, and physical danger was the habitual exhilaration that kept him alive in spite of his lack of desire. He treated her kindly because she puzzled him, and he never trifled with mysteries but always maltreated them, or bowed

to them, according to their ability at censuring him
without making him irritated.

Jessica was sitting with him one night in a
"bohemian" tea room that was steeped in a kind
of garish ghastliness, and trying to prevent him
from fighting a group of college boys at an adjoining table, while he assimilated his favorite drug and
uttered truculent remarks. The hour was 2 A.M.,
and the only other people in the place were the
college youths, an insipid-faced chorus girl, and her
fat, dully elderly escort. Suddenly, Sariman crashed
down upon the table, his arms dangling and his head
buried in a brass flower-bowl with several nas-
turtiums hanging down from the sides of his head.
After a moment of thickening silence, the place became agitated, and the proprietor, a middle-aged,
furtive-faced, Balkan Jew, ran up with cold water
and towels for Sariman's head. The place rang
with excited instructions—"Make him drink some
vinegar!", "Bathe his feet in warm water—that's
always good!", "Take his collar off and let him
breathe!"—while Jessica, who thought that he had
merely fainted, aided the others in their efforts to
restore him and wearily faced the onerous task of
transporting him to his rooms. In the meantime,
some one had hastened to the street and summoned
a policeman, and the policeman stalked in and examined Sariman. Then he straightened up and
frowned.

"This man's dead," he said. "Do you get me?—

he's dead. There's something funny about this. You're all material witnesses and you'll all have to stay here till the city physician comes and looks him over. It looks like a damn suspicious case to me!" Every one in the place became still and silent, for a dramatic, unexpected fear can demolish the effects of whisky in an instant, and each person stared at the other as though he had been an unwitting accomplice in the death of this man and would probably hang for it. The most salient trait of innocent people, when they are abruptly confronted by accusing eyes, is to act as though they were unmistakably guilty—a fact that often misleads amateur detectives and stupid crime-ferreters —for they are apt to be shocked at the thought that they may be charged with a crime which they did not commit, and they lack the guilty person's reasons for self-control.

The policeman, a corpulent man with a ruddy, stolid face, ordered the proprietor to lock the doors and then telephoned to his station, with a report of the case. He returned to Jessica and shot questions at her, which concerned her name, residence, occupation, and how she happened to be with the dead man, and what had transpired before his death. Jessica had been staring down at Sariman's corpse, with a torpid incredulity, all of her thoughts suspended and hushed. There was some odd mistake—he couldn't be dead; it was too appalling to consider. Then the essence of final, clammy cessation, which hangs over a dead man and makes him different from one who is merely sleeping, touched Jessica and made her shrink.   Death—what a harshly venomous, inexplicable, ruthless thing it was, and how it pounced upon the evanescent animations of human beings and made them seem to be only past shivers of imagination. It was impossible for her to feel any emotion toward Sariman except a surprised and reflective envy—he was better situated now than she who sat beside his meaningless body in this sordid, disturbed tea room and waited to be cross-examined by inane human beings.

When the policeman commenced his questions, her mind came back to life, and she had the alertness of one who spies the tiniest of traps ahead of him and eludes them, more from force of habit than from any real dread. If they discovered that he had taken heroin in the tea room, they would insist upon connecting her with his death and she would have to pass through a harried, protesting turmoil to regain her freedom—a hideous prospect, of no service to the dead man beside her. She responded to the questions with an earnest and guileless air—yes, she was a friend of Sariman, nothing else, and he had been drinking heavily during the night, and he had told her once that he suffered from a weak heart. The college boys whispered to each other in a shaken manner and acted as though they longed to leap through one of the windows, and the shrewdly baby-faced chorus girl was in a nervous

furore, and moved her lips as though she were praying to a God whom she had forgotten, and did not
know what words to use, and the elderly business
man beside her began to bluster and demand that
he be released.

Two plainclothes men arrived and took the place
of the policeman, who returned to his beat, and they
resumed the questioning for a time. They had
noticed an expensive limousine parked in front of
the place and when they discovered that Jessica was
the owner, they treated her with a cautious polite-
ness—these rich bugs could make it hot for you if
you tried to put anything over on them. Silence
returned to the tea room, and everyone except Jessica fidgeted, and whispered, and boldly strove to
induce the detectives to release them, and acted as
if the dead man so near at hand had reminded them
of the impermanence of life and they were afraid
that it would be their turn next. They tried not
to look at him, but their eyes came back to him with
a regular fascination.

Jessica began to feel that the dead man was
rigidly reproaching her—she had watched him take
the heroin without making any effort to prevent
him—and she shrank back against the wall and
miserably longed to join him and explain to him
that she had not realized what the consequences of
their night would be. Then her reason asserted
itself and asked her why any one should stop another
person from dying, if he wanted to—was life so

intrinsically radiant and valuable that a few years more or less of it meant everything? If death signified a more powerful continuation of your individuality, then life was only an unimportant obstruction, and if it meant simply the grave and worms, then life was an equally flitting jest. Still, her emotions recoiled from the corpse beside her and gave her an uneasiness which she could not conquer, or analyze.

Dawn crept slowly into the tea room, freshly oblivious to the people within it, and the inert mold of flesh stiffening over a table—the tea room was on the second story of a building, with its windows facing the street. The chorus girl and the elderly man had fallen asleep; the college boys still talked in low tones about their predicament—"What the hell can they do to us, we didn't know him"—and the detectives discussed the case with each other and scanned the others with a never-relenting suspicion. Jessica had dropped into a wide-eyed stupor, in which the entire scene had become unreal and dismally void of significance.

When the city physician arrived, however, she straightened up and grew warily attentive—this portly, tired-faced, half-stupid man had the power to restrict and harass her immediate future. After he had questioned her, and examined the dead man, he telephoned to a sister of Sariman—Jessica had given him the number. He returned to Jessica, from the booth telephone, and said, in the presence of the detectives: "It's a plain case of heart failure. His sister tells me that he almost passed out two months ago from a heart attack, and she's hurrying down now. Sorry we had to hold you overnight, Miss Maringold, but you know, we've got to be careful about these things. Of course, there's no necessity of your remaining now. You must be in a frightful nervous state, and I'd advise you to stick to your bed for the next day or two, and take it easy."

He had a vague remembrance of having heard the name, Jessica Maringold, in connection with society and charitable affairs, and he was profusely cordial. Jessica almost ran from the tea room, with a feeling of aching relief.

Afterwards, as she repulsed the reporters who sought to waylay her for interviews, and read the newspaper accounts of the episode, with captions such as: "Young Multi-Millionairess With Sariman Before His Death, Police Exonerate Her," she felt sickened, and cheapened, and self-hating—the thought that she had been a jauntily selfish accomplice of Death persisted in spite of her logic, and the publicity made her feel as though she were bound and gagged under a spotlight. Her mood was aggravated still more by a visit from Sariman's mother—for some reason that can only be psychic, belligerent rakes nearly always spring from ultra-respectable families—and the mother, a stalwart, sour-faced woman, had given vent to hysterical denunciations and had cried: "It was you and your kind that killed him—don't tell me, I know!" Disgusted and aimless, Jessica fled to Europe, where she drifted from one capital to another, and took care to have only the most casual relations with people whom she met at hotels and restaurants, and resumed her painting with the feeling: "I'm not really a creator but I might as well play at being one, since everything else has died down." Sex had become an exploited, unrewarding nuisance that lead to melodramas, and quarrels, and ennuis, and she shunned it with a tactful proficiency.

At the end of the year she wound up in London, and rented an apartment in Chelsea, close to the one in which she had previously lived. She visited the "1919 Club" and found that most of the old faces were gone—Chamberlain had married and was sojourning in Paris, and Israel was attached to a government commission in Palestine—but she was recognized by Caswell, Cecelia's former friend, and once more installed as an honorary member. She paid a dutiful call to the Swinsons, and after a few hours of measureless, defenseless boredom in their midst, she resolved not to see them again. To wring pleasantries, and regards, and tattling responses from the emptiness of her spirit was a dispiriting feat that could not be repeated, and the Swinsons themselves felt that her wealth had made her too uppish and self-intrenched—she always seemed to be laughing at them, in spite of her careful graciousness, and they had no desire to be secretly patronized as poor relations when they were every whit as good as she was!

At the "1919 Club," Jessica met a young American named Arnold Dowley—an expatriated poet-wastrel who lived through the favors and whims of other people, whom he attracted by his wit, his piano-playing abilities, his metaphorical declarations of love, if the prospect was a woman—anything that could insure his food and lodging for another week. Hearing that Jessica was a wealthy, unmarried woman, he courted her "accidentally," finding out where she was apt to be and appearing at the place with a surprised gratitude at having met her again (wealthy women usually didn't like to feel that you were deliberately and assiduously pursuing them, unless you belonged to their station in life). His instinct told him to be quite frank and unadorned with her, for underneath her genial poise she always seemed to say, without uttering the words: "Don't waste your time in maneuvering and protesting, but tell me what you want of me."

He had a short, slight, almost feminine body, and a drooping, pallid face—that not quite brown color, in which dusk and dawn find each other—and the smallest of lips always parted a bit, and an upturned nose below his hopeless, black eyes, and a tangle of brownish black hair. He adapted his manners to those of the person whom he was accompanying, but when he had no reason to be on guard he revealed a tranquil pessimism that had once been bitterness and had found it to be tiresome. Jessica liked him because he seemed close to what she would have been if wealth had not protected her—a spuriously humble, super-vagabond, trading a false image of herself to this person and that, for the dubious relief of daubing paint on canvas, and avenging herself by tricking and injuring the least sincere among her benefactors. He had a talent for writing sad, thistledown verse that was never trite or original, but vaguely reminiscent of other men's poems.

With a despairing candor, he asked her to give him money—a weekly allowance—so that he could continue to tinker with the piano and his verses.

"You're burdened with money and I have none of it," he said. "About the only thing that I want from life is the chance to be thoughtfully lazy and to improvise with a few words, and a few chords, before I die. The rest doesn't matter—one night of drinking and another of love-making, and another of gay words and piano thumpings, and all to persuade life to let me live. It becomes more and more difficult with every year, but it's better than trudging from some office around Fleet Street. There's an immense charm in knowing that you can rise in the morning whenever you please and twiddle your fingers at life."

Jessica gave him the money with an unconcerned spirit—it meant everything to him and it was a bothersome over-abundance to her, and the only people from whom she felt inclined to withhold it were those who elaborately schemed for it, or those who wanted it for mundane objects. She would have given a thousand dollars to one who wanted to purchase an incredibly valuable rose, but not to one who was longing for an automobile.

Her relations with Dowley were unruffled and companionable until he began to make love to her. Her sensuous, ultra-sophisticated detachment from the major greeds and vanities of life became a strengthening presence which he found himself more and more unable to dispense with. If she deserted his life, he would have to go back to his old pretenses, and squirmings, and hired exuberances, and humiliations with people whose natures were infinitely smaller than Jessica's, or who desired a deeply steady emotion which he could not give them. The once inevitable game slowly took on the quality of an impending nightmare, which he had evaded for the first time but which still hung over him. He did not dare to ask Jessica to marry him, for fear that she would be inexorably tempted to suspect his motives, but he begged her to let him live with her and to remain in England.

"I don't want to spoil it with sex," she said to him one night, as they sat in her apartment. "I've never given myself to a man yet without killing the fine, sensitive edge of our relations with each other. It seems to tell you: 'Well, you've both sunk to a woman and her man now, and you'll have to stick to that and leave your pretty vaporings about each other, and wait for the abrupt and disagreeable end to come along——it always does !'   I don't say that I'm going to be ascetic for the rest of my life, but I'll always look upon sex with a feeling of dread and distrust——I've had too much of it.   I'll leave you enough money to live on for the rest of your days, Arniboy, and I'll trot about with you as long as I'm in England, but I can't honestly promise you anything else."

As he reflected, he knew that material security was only a secondary part of his motives, and that his life would become barren and disquieted without the closeness of her encouragement and understanding. He was not self-sufficient, and he had always gambled for the attention of people whom he needed and despised at the same time, but Jessica increased this need tenfold and took the compensation of dislike away from him, so that he was left alone and unprotected in her absence.   Other people were so fettered, and purposelessly cruel, and unseeing in comparison to her.

"I don't want your money," he answered, wearily. "I could still get it from other people.   I'd have to lie, and scamper, and stand on my head for it, of course, but it wouldn't be impossible if that were all I cared for.   There's a delicate, unquestioning, and, oh, almost serene reward in being with you, and if I lose it, Jes', I'll become too weak to go back to the old, endless plotting and grimacing.   I'm just as tired of sex as you are, and I want to escape from smirking and prattling to one woman after another, and from telling her the things she'd like to hear, without showing her that I know she'd like to hear them."

"You're making a tragedy out of a fancy," she replied. "If you lived with me you'd become restless, and ill tempered, and argumentative inside of six months. The dream would just change to a little, annoying convenience, and you'd see crowds of whims and irritations in me that you'd never noticed before. Besides, if you don't have to worry about money after I'm gone, then you can stop all of your caperings to other women, and act as you please."

He went on with his pleading and she clung to her light contradictions. Then, several days later, after she had told him that she was leaving England in a week, he failed to keep an appointment with her, and when she sought him at his rooming house, she found that he had killed himself on the previous evening. First shocked, and then limply downcast, she kept to her apartment for the next two days and did little but sit and stare at the walls. Dowley haunted her with the most pensive and child-like of rebukes, and she seemed to sense his still hands forever held out to her with an unassuming and trusting request. She had tried to help him and had only tormented him with a first refuge that had been threatened by recurring emptiness, and she had interrupted all of his half supplicating and half derisive flings with life and made him unable to lift his

feet again. Why couldn't human beings cut themselves into similar, flesh-and-blood entities and leave
one behind with each begging person—there never
seemed to be any other solution. Perhaps one of
the blessings of a Hereafter—if there was one—
would be that each spirit could divide itself into
numbers of identical but detached individualities,
and thus refrain from senselessly injuring the other
spirits who craved its presence and being. She began to whisper, feverishly explaining sentences to
Dowley, as though he were seated beside her, and
she debated with herself on the question of whether
she was immensely selfish or merely a woman of rov-
ing impulses whose kindness was slain by the fact
that they could never remain still.

This second connection with the death of a man
placed her in a gravely apprehensive mood, and she
returned to New York with the determination to
immerse herself in some methodical, useful labor and
stop her disastrous philanderings with men. She attached herself to an East-Side settlement house—a
prim, officiously charitable, undiscriminating place,
where she was joyously welcomed because of the
gain and notoriety that sprang from having a million-
airess as a teacher of the children. She formed a
class of the more precocious children and instructed
them in drawing and painting, and watched their
squinting absorptions and answered their shrewdly
groping questions with the first pangs of motherly
feeling that she had ever known. She had said to

herself again and again that eventually she wanted
to have at least one child, because it would perpet-
uate her thwarted struggle against life, but her reactions had been more mental than emotional, and
she had felt no immediate, tantalizing urge to give
birth to one. Subconsciously, she had shrunk from
the pain and self-obliteration of motherhood, with
its attendant loss of physical symmetries, but the
sexual and artistic distractions of her life had
strengthened this fear without compelling her to
recognize it. If she had been thrown upon a lonely
island, with a man acceptable to her emotions, the
question of being a mother would have pressed upon
her, but in the ease and freedom of her life it failed
to disturb her, and her quarrels with Purrel had been
resentful avoidances of the subject. She had coolly
used methods of birth prevention, with the thought
that "there was plenty of time" and that she wanted
to drain and explore her own life before giving another life to the earth.

Now, the steady nearness of these children in her
class, with their appealing innocences and fidgeting
dawns of introspection, made her long to conceive
a child of her own and guide its life—something like
restoring a number of her mistakes, and former
hopes, and searches, in another being, and making
them a little less blundering or having at least the
enjoyment of watching a qualified reproduction of
her own fight with life. The honored ecstasy of
hugging a baby-head against her breast, with its

softened and prostrate disguise of selfish instincts, was foreign to her anticipations, for she felt that only unimaginative women could drool, and slobber, and croon over their children, but she did desire to embrace a child of her own, with the feeling that she was wisely and sadly protecting a severed part of herself until it grew up and was able to face the confusions, and aches, and malices of a world. She wanted to fondle it as though she were stroking her own bruises with a conscious selfishness. As she looked at the children who clustered about her—all of them under fifteen—with their soft faces already drawn and beaten by the coarse vehemences of life in tenement houses, and as she listened to their bursts of billingsgate picked up from their elders on the street, she longed to let at least one, new life escape from being kicked, and tricked, and defiled during its most beseeching years.

One day she took her class to a huge, public art museum, where they sat on camp stools which they had brought with them and sketched sculptured objects, and carved relics, and ancient costumes. It was necessary for them to leave their belongings in the basement of the museum, and rows of metal lockers had been installed there, since the museum was visited each day by sketch classes and people who desired to copy some of the old masterpieces among the paintings. A man sat at a desk near the lockers and gave out the keys, and accepted a small fee for each one, and guarded objects of exceptional value in a drawer of the desk, and rented easels to applicants. He was a tall, bony, crippled man, and the left side of his torso was paralyzed, with the left arm doubled-up and the hand drooping down from the wrist in a twisted fashion, while his left leg was a little shorter than the right. The straight line of his nose ended between brown eyes that were huge in their proportion to the rest of his long face, and his lips were thinly compressed, and he had a large, brown mustache, and a brown beard that almost extended to his chest. His clothes were dark and ill-fitting, and they increased his serenely somber aspect, and if a halo had circled his head it would not have violated the reality of his appearance.

Immersed in the demands of her children, Jessica gave him glances of perfunctory curiosity, but when she saw that he was reading "Education Sentimentale," by Flaubert, she sent her children ahead and stopped to speak to him.

"Doesn't it weary you to sit here all day in this gloomy, musty basement?" she asked, moved to speak directly to him without knowing why, except that she had a touch of inquisitive pity.

He waited ten seconds before answering, and looked at her with a shifting frown on his pale face.

"You were attracted by the book I'm reading," he said. "It's not usually read by museum attendants. But still, you may be making a mistake. I saw a girl reading Browning once, in a subway car, and when I spoke to her she said that she had to read 'the darned, old thing' to keep up in her English classes and it was giving her a headache."

Jessica became nonplused at the thought that she had uttered what must have sounded like a patronizing kindness to a man whose mind might be far keener than her own.

"I suppose I've hurt you a bit," she said. "I always seem to hurt people without meaning to. Tell me, what makes you sit in this basement from morning to night and hand out keys? Is it poverty?"

"Yes, that, and my crippled condition," he answered. "Besides, I've been writing a book on æsthetic criticism and painting, and it's easier to work on it in this quiet place—the duties here don't take up much of my time. I've been here three years now, and this basement fits into my spirit— a dark, solid, stiffly subtle place in spite of its plain walls and floor. It doesn't ask you to notice it and it doesn't encourage you to become sentimental."

Jessica was intrigued by his instantly confidential way of speaking, and the probing sadness of his words.

"Do you always talk so freely to strange people?" she asked.

"Either that, or I remain silent," he answered. "When you sit in a silent basement from morning to twilight, spoken words become a startling gift indeed, and you weigh them in your head, reluctant to let them go, and you don't care to give them to

every one. Once in a great while an instinct tells me
to say more than yes and no to some person who
comes in here, and it's usually a wrong one, but it
bobs up regularly."

"Well, I'd like to show you that it's not so frightfully wrong in my case," Jessica said, smiling, liking
his modulated candor that drew near to sentimentality and checked itself one step away from this
quality. What tortures might be within him, inducing him softly to lessen them in his speech? She
was approaching sentimentality herself! What was
there in this still unknown man that could cause
such a change?

"I've got to go up to the children now but I'm
coming back to-morrow afternoon," she said. "We
haven't even begun to talk to each other."

He told her his name—Ernest Maller—and she
gave him her own.

She visited him on the next day, and he read her
extracts from his book manuscript and talked of his
past life. He had been crippled since his boyhood,
and his mother had taken care of him until he was
twenty-five—he had been the only child and his
father had died years ago. Then his mother became ill and went to the grave, leaving him with a
scant three thousand dollars, which he had lived on
until the end of it had forced him to accept the
museum job. He had written articles on art and
architecture for different magazines, but they failed
to give him a sufficient and regular income. He

spoke of his past with a ruthless, despairing calmness, as though he were treading on the graves of emotions that had once been morbid and maudlin at different times.

As Jessica continued to visit him in his basement—he refused to see her elsewhere because he said that other backgrounds would be more embarrassing to him—she became more and more receptive to his shadowed and yet strenuous mind—a paradox that is often contained in men whose physical weakness rebukes their thoughts and makes these thoughts redouble their activities—and to the emotions that had grown sturdy and self-possessed to counteract his hesitant and partly distorted body. His chief faults were a querulous self-mockery, which he sometimes reiterated until it became too much like the wearisome complaints of a self-conscious child, and a tendency to look at everything with a rigidly æsthetic bias, but Jessica felt that these were flaws which his life had inevitably thrust upon him.

At first she pitied his physical condition, and thus suppressed her mild aversion to it, but by degrees she began to welcome it as something that she could hold up, and nourish. Her depleted sensual desires relished the idea of lending themselves to a man who would be dependent upon them without overtaxing them. It seemed to her that she had always taken much from men, giving them little in return because they had been unable to see or touch the greater part of her, and here was a chance to reverse the process, physically at least.

Maller loved her, but he had vowed to himself that he would never court her. She gave him the feeling of a semi-gargoyle, who had hopped down from the top of a cathedral and was speaking to an understanding and deliberately tolerant woman on the pavement below. He was obsessed by the idea that his body was repugnant to her, against her will, and that she listened intently to his words, in an effort to forget this repugnance, but never quite succeeded.

One afternoon, as they sat and talked in the basement of the museum, a decisive impulse came to Jessica, and she said: "Will you marry me, Ernest?" in the casually inquiring manner of one to whom the other person's assent was inevitable. He frowned and remained silent for a full minute.

"Yes, I know, you pity me, and you want to take care of me, and you'd like to be selfish in a way that you've never tried before—an unbending, melting way," he said. "You don't see that you'd only be hitting me, and disrupting me, with every one of your caresses, and all of your favors and attentions."

Then, the first emotional certainty that she had ever known came to her.

"I love you, Ernest," she answered, with a controlled voice, and as she uttered the phrase she recalled that she had never before spoken it to any

other man. The other men in her life had replen-
ished her egotism without assaulting it sufficiently
to make it pliant to their desires, and a crippled,
partially helpless man had reduced it to that point
where it could prostrate itself before him but still
retain its identity. An instinctive conviction dismissed his doubts, and his right hand rose to her
shoulder.

THE END